GW01048669

YOUR SICK

YOUR SICK

STORIES

ELIZABETH J. COLEN
CAROL GUESS
KELLY MAGEE

Layout and Cover Design by Justin Lawrence Daugherty
Cover Image: by Holly Andres

ISBN: 978-0-9967823-2-6; 978-0-9967823-3-3

Produced and printed in the United States of America.

CONTENTS

FORGETTING WENDY

You left our baby on the bus.

I know; you were texting. Almost missed your stop. Squeezed past grocery bags and knapsacks, guitars and guide dogs. Wendy Jean Stephanie slept swaddled in an organic cotton blanket covered with red and green parrots, forgotten in the window seat. No one could believe you'd left your infant, so they assumed she wasn't yours. Someone dialed 911 to report a baby living large on the bus.

When you walked through the door, I knew. Our eyes met, and it was the reverse of the first time our eyes met, strangers. Our eyes met, and I knew you'd forgotten our baby. She wasn't across town with your mom or out of sight in her swing. She was somewhere else, in the wide world without us. You gasped as if drowning and raced out the door.

Forty minutes later you called from the corner of Broadway and Pine, where you'd spoken to the officer in charge and everything, you said, was fine.

I screamed Fuck you and Your fault if she's dead. Then I drove to the station, where a blue coat held Wendy against bulletproof glass.

Interviews with CPS. Paperwork and a home visit. She was ours the next morning because accidents happen. Everyone said so, especially you.

That night you nursed her on the sofa while we watched our shows. I made pasta because it was my turn to make pasta.

Don't tell Dan, you said, slurping spaghetti. As if donor

dad might ask for his sperm back.

A few weeks later you were reading and got up to answer the phone. When I came home I found you raking leaves in the yard, Wendy lolling unattended on the sofa. Then you went grocery shopping and left a cart full of Wendy in the cereal aisle.

You remembered everything else in precise detail. You gave lectures on law, history, art. You remembered how much each utility bill cost and the name of the paint we used on the porch. You remembered birthdays and anniversaries, obscure song lyrics and political speeches. You remembered my body and how I like to be touched: the precise angle of wrist, the curve of your mouth.

Sometimes we woke in the middle of the night, Wendy warm and round between us. When I carried her in the sling, she swung. She bit pacifiers into shredded plastic. Later, she rode the dog like a horse.

You got tested: above average IQ, even though you called the hippo a rhino during the oral. Dr. Zulaski called it "mom brain" and chuckled. Friends suggested setting alerts on your phone: Check for daughter! or, Forgetting Wendy? Tattoo her name on your palm. Tie a ribbon around your finger. Get her chipped, like a puppy.

They turned you into a fixable thing, but I refused to downplay the danger. I said, "What if you left Wendy in a hot car? In the bathtub?" I became a single parent to two, baby and you, and my workload doubled. I demanded curfews and receipts. Banned you from the stove. Bought you a strap-on carrier so when you took the baby with you, you had to wear her.

Wendy slept soundly in her crib, but you began waking at night, groping for her in the sheets. "I can't find her," you'd cry and you'd fight me if I tried to help. One night I said, "I've got her," and you froze, eyes closed, cradling linen.

"You have Wendy?"

"She's with me."

You began to cry. I knew you were awake, though the next morning you denied it. "What if I don't love her enough?"

"You love her enough," I said because what else was I going to say.

You relaxed back. "Don't leave us, okay? We need you."

I smoothed your brow. I promised not to leave because I thought you'd get better. The kind of promise that binds people who have already lost each other.

When Wendy got old enough to have a preference, she chose lost over found. The two of you broke curfew at the zoo, snapping photographs of tropical birds clinging to nets, gorillas with glassy stares. Look what we brought you, Wendy would say when you returned, trotting out picture after picture of captivity. Wendy would laugh about your forgetting, and the laughter became a kind of acceptance: She tried to leave me at the arcade. I let her get all the way to the exit before I stopped her.

You: vindicated and all smiles.

But later, when Wendy called me from a gas station an hour away, or when she walked in sweaty and exhausted three hours late from an environmental club meeting, or when I got calls from the cops, there would be no affection in her voice. I wouldn't ask questions and I wouldn't offer explanations. You'd still be gone then, or you'd be asleep in our bed, and Wendy would stand in the doorway watching.

Sometimes you apologized before you opened your eyes.

Sometimes you startled awake and didn't recognize us.

Sometimes you gathered the sheets in your arms and rocked.

Our daughter watched you, wondering what it meant. I watched her, wondering what the cost.

Wendy brought home worksheets about the life cycle of salmon and the difference between threatened and endangered. She told us she didn't want to eat meat, and she wanted to quit environmental club and join Junior-PETA instead. She knew changes in schedule were bad for you; that was why she did it. You kept showing up to environmental club and texting me in a panic. Wendy gave me the names of the families she caught rides with, and they all sounded like dog breeds: the Schnauzers, the Labradors. Straight married couples with hybrid cars, kids with game addictions. Normal: she was trying it on. You kept making her plates of chicken and pork chops; she told us gruesome stories of cage-cannibalism. You could remember what I'd ordered at a restaurant three years ago, but never anything Wendy told you.

When she stopped talking to you, she stopped talking to me, too.

I didn't blame you for what we eventually called your illness. I didn't leave you. But I did forget to tell you things. The late-night emails to an old high school friend in Florida. The confessions: too much, too lonely, too far. The meetings I told you were in different cities, which were all really the same city.

I told you I needed space, but I forgot to tell you that space had a name. Heidi. She was considering changing it. She was considering becoming someone entirely different.

Heidi didn't believe in forgetting. Some people have babies to save a relationship, she said. When that doesn't work, they try other things.

At Heidi's place, there were no DO NOT FORGET lists in panicked script. It was another universe, where we could be anyone we wanted. When I was there, you and Wendy receded into the haze of a life I remembered from long ago. Until you texted in the middle of the night.

Are you there?

I'm here. Wendy?

Hold on.

I would wait, imagining you bumping down the hallway to her room. Planning, as I always did, for what I would do if it was empty.

She's here. Goodnight.

Goodnight.

When Wendy turned twelve, she began taking the city bus to school. Her lunch box was tagged with graffiti. She was cool already, out of our league. Moms, she'd say, exasperated, when we tried to dress her, when we gave her stuffed animals. I like boys, she sighed, when we dragged her to Pride. She gave the eye to grown men. Flirted with Dan.

When she turned fifteen she got invited to junior prom. You drove her and her date to the high school gym. Watched while Wayne Mustard pinned her corsage.

I was visiting my family in Florida, where my parents had retired to a condo overlooking the beach. This was the lie I told to keep peace. In truth I was visiting my ex, Heidi, who'd changed her name and her hormones to Hank.

Hank lived in Brooklyn, in a tiny apartment with three roommates, all working different shifts, hot-bunking two beds. We had sex while Freddie and Shannon were waiting tables and Mina was walking the community dog. My phone kept blinking; I could tell it was you. I called back and you answered and I asked about Wendy. "How was the prom?"

Your silence told me you'd forgotten. You hung up, and I pictured you driving recklessly across bridges and bike lanes, racing to school where she sat on the stoop.

Except when you got to Crown Hill High School of Internet Arts and Sciences there was no sign of her.

"Call the police," I yelled, stuffing clothes into my suitcase. "I'm catching the first flight home."

Before I turned off my phone I noticed Wendy had sent me a text.

Photo: Wendy standing next to an elephant, high heels and prom dress glowing deep green. Yellow roses drooped from her wrist. Wayne Mustard hovered, matching green cummerbund.

The flight home was a blur of dire thoughts and disbelief. Was it more my fault than yours? Because I knew your way with forgetting. Because what you forgot became more mine than yours. I envisioned Wendy riding a zebra, bottle-feeding a lion, racing wild dogs.

When the plane touched tarmac I turned on my phone. A little blue icon told me you'd texted.

I can't believe you lied about Heidi.

Not a word about Wendy.

You'd forgotten again.

I drove past the high school on my way to the zoo. The slick metal doors mocked me with their technological savvy. Inside were students tangled in cords, tweeting tiny poems, writing code that could find or lose anyone. They wore glasses that doubled as screens, and fluttered their lashes in new Morse code.

When I pulled into the parking lot of the Woodland Park Zoo, I recognized a few of Wendy's friends, dressed for prom, but picketing the zoo. They stuffed flyers into purses and knapsacks, under wheels and windshield wipers.

You would've been proud, but you weren't here. Wendy and Wayne Mustard were standing outside, holding a sagging banner that read: FREE THE ELEPHANTS! I stepped in to help. I lifted the "FREE."

ZERO FEVER

My girl had a fever. My boy stayed cool, but my girl burned. I kept watch while they slept, girl on the bottom bunk because I worried she'd fall. The bunk beds were my ex's idea; my ex was gone, but the carpentry stayed. It was just the three of us and an underwater mortgage. I explained to the kids that the bank owned the house.

"But the bank doesn't live here," Zachary frowned.

Zara said *house* and *water* and *please.*

Day three of sick, and she still had a fever. While Zack was in school I drove to the hospital. The doctor took one look at Zara and gestured me into the hall alone.

"Tell me the truth."

He looked down at his clipboard.

"She's been sick for three days."

He coughed into his sleeve. "You do know Zara's a parrot?"

It seemed so cruel of him, standing there all tall and human, language flying from his mouth, little colored lines I puzzled together. *Everything loves,* I thought; *birds and plants and your stupid fucking golf ball tie.*

"I'm aware."

"Of course."

He gave me the name of a veterinarian. I explained that Zara was closer to human than bird, that anything making her sick was a human disease, but he wouldn't listen.

At the vet's office they sent us back to the hospital. We'd

gone back and forth like this before: stranded in the waiting room, red feathers and the chair on fire.

"There's a doctor downtown," the man beside me whispered. "Second and Cherry. Doctor Zulaski." He opened his wallet and showed me a photo. "My first born, my parrot. My beautiful girl."

The fever clung to Zara's wings. She pulled out her feathers, nipped at her feet. Finally I mixed children's Tylenol into her seeds. I didn't know what else to do.

That night my ex came over for Family Dinner. We talked about the secret network that existed in whispers, gestures, glances at bird baths. Then we fucked, which I knew we'd regret when it was cold in our separate beds across town.

Scientists still didn't know what caused it. I blamed the organic eggs I'd eaten, the free-range chicken. It was an epidemic with a fancy scientific name, but everyone called it Zero Fever. One day Zara was an adorable human toddler; the next day, a bird with red and green wings. There was nothing gradual about the change. I remember hearing strange sounds from the nursery, opening the door, stepping into her flight path.

Sometimes baby birds turned back. Videos of transformation racked up hits on YouTube. Some were staged; a few looked real. I studied the real ones, desperate for clues. I had to believe my girl would return.

Scientists were working to cure it. Celebrities wore red and green bracelets, ran marathons to benefit non-profits. Beneath the booming metropolis of illness was a conspiracy theory. Sometimes I went online and clicked the links. Talk of changelings and midnight abductions. Talk of stealing and exchange. After all, no one had ever seen their child turn into a parrot. In every instance, a parent opened the door to their child's room; out flew a bewildered bird. No sign of the child, just feathers and glass. Zero Fever, perhaps. Or a ladder, perched against the house, and a bird left in place of a baby.

I fell in love with my parrot-child. I let her be Zara, until she was more real than Zara, until my human baby was only memory. Until I was consumed with bird.

I joined a group of activist parents, petitioning to let parrot children enroll in school.

I spoke out against the search for a cure, and spoke instead of embracing difference.

I didn't tell anyone I suspected there might be two Zaras: my human child, stolen; and my talkative bird, loved now but missing from some faraway forest.

I tried not to think of words like *sex trade* or *slave labor* or *illegal adoption.* I had nightmares of my human girl calling for me in a parrot voice.

Zara had nightmares, too. She woke with a rattle in her throat, saying *baby* and *fly* and *dark.* I crept to her side, felt for her chest. The musk of fever hung over the bed. Her heartbeat thudded against my fingers. "Zara?" I whispered.

Hot, she said.

I felt my way out of the room and left a message for my ex, then called Dr. Zulaski's answering service. While I waited for him to call back, I returned to the kids' room. Zack was sitting up on the top bunk, flashlight in hand.

"Who were you talking to?" he said.

"Shh," I said. "The doctor. I'm worried about your sister."

He leaned over the edge and shined the light on her before I could tell him not to wake her. She didn't wake. She lay panting on her pillow, beak open, a wet spot on the sheet near her mouth.

"Whoa," Zack said.

"Zara?" I slid a hand under her body. My phone buzzed in my pocket. "She's unconscious," I said, first to the room and then into the phone. Dr. Zulaski said he'd meet us there. I picked her up, my tiny, limp girl. A patch of feathers on the bedspread. Blue and green falling from my arms.

The thought didn't escape me. In the car, hope ran parallel to fear.

Transformation.

Based on the YouTube videos and my own dreams, here's what I thought would happen: her feathers would fall out. The skin underneath would be covered in downy hair, enough to constitute a pelt. Still animal, but closer now to mammal. She'd stretch and retract her wings, stretch and stretch, and from wings would come arms. From claws, toes. She wouldn't shed her bird entirely, but the human would prevail.

Or maybe I'd open the door and she'd be returned, just as she was.

One of the great dangers, parents of so-called "cured" children wrote, was the recovered human-child's obsession with heights.

Based on what actually happened, I no longer watch YouTube

videos.

Dr. Zulaski had a feline way of moving, thick hands, eyes framed by golden eyebrows and bushy hair. He fixed his gaze on me in a way that was unsettling, but he seemed to know what he was doing. He took Zara's vitals and scratched notes on a chart.

"Tylenol, you say?" He nudged a back door open with his foot and whistled into the hall. "How much?"

A tall nurse with big teeth and bedhead pushed a metal cart into the room. Dr. Z handed her the chart, and she wheeled Zara out.

"I don't know," I said. "Not much. I didn't know what else to do. No one would help me."

Dr. Z gave me the same heavy, golden stare. "It's a shame. Animals are children, too."

Zack had curled up on the bench seat in the exam room, and he lifted his head. Dr. Z's eyes flicked toward the movement; he hadn't noticed Zack before. The doctor visibly smoothed himself and smiled. "You have another."

"This is my son, Zack," I said.

"I took it away from her," Zack said.

"Took what, honey?"

"The Tylenol." He pursed his lips. "You should know better, Mom."

Dr. Z's eyes darted between us. He seemed less like a man than an animal carrying human baggage.

"A mistake," I faltered.

"To be clear," Dr. Z stood to leave, "Zara has not ingested anything unusual."

I looked at Zack.

"She might've eaten some of it," he said. "But I took the rest away."

Dr. Z wanted to keep Zara for observation. My ex pulled into the parking lot as we exited. I gave him the short version and asked if he'd stay with Zara. Zack held onto my hand like he was prepared to fight for it.

My ex kissed my cheek and stayed.

Zack was quiet in the car. I tucked him into my bed, something he didn't permit often anymore. As I turned out the light, he said, "Mom, Zara is a parrot."

"And you are my boy," I said.

"I mean," he propped himself on his elbows. "If we'd bought her at the pet store, you wouldn't have given her people medicine."

I often suspected my kids understood everything—illness, adulthood, me—better than I did.

"You have to know that she's a bird." His voice wavered. "You have to know it."

"Zara is a bird and your sister," I said. "I need to remember that."

He relaxed back onto his pillow. "Yes," he said.

I listened to him fall asleep, felt the unraveling of his thought and attention and consciousness. I waited for the nightmare that I knew would come to him, and when it did, I put my hand on his forehead and smoothed it away.

I didn't sleep. I texted my ex for news, but there wasn't any for a long time, and he assured me that was good. I opened my computer and dared myself to look them up, the YouTube videos. To repeat the search for "cured." To open the photo file marked with her name. To look for signs from the past that might predict the future.

I loved my parrot-child, and most of the time, there was enough love for both Zaras, the one I had and the one I mourned. But sometimes, in the middle of the night, I longed for my human-child. My baby. I wanted her in my arms, pulling my hair with opposable thumbs.

Dr. Z called with good and bad news. Zara was fine, he said. She responded well to the fluids and was up and about.

"And the bad news?" I said.

He didn't mince words; I respected him for it. "She looks different."

"The feather loss?"

"No." Animal noises burst in and out behind him. "You'll find that she's quite changed. But she's still the same Zara inside."

I texted my ex: *?*

He texted back: *!*

Transition, I thought. My baby, I thought. My heart leapt on the drive to the clinic, Zack scowling in the back seat. I lived an entire recovery in the course of that ride. Grief became a thing I used to feel. I arrived at the clinic a new person.

But then doubt set in. Dr. Z called us back from a waiting room filled with sick animals. Parrots, lemurs, tamarins, frogs. I wondered how many of them were kids with Zero Fever. How many animals with real fevers. I looked at the faces of the parents, wondered if it mattered to them which was which. We lived in this world where animals might be babies and everyone acted accordingly, which was maybe good for the humans, but plenty bad for the animals. *Everything grieves*, I thought. *Parrots and babies and empty waiting room chairs.*

I held Zack's hand and followed Dr. Z down the hall. I couldn't help hoping for human, just as I knew Zack was hoping for bird. Our sorrow, our hope, kept reinventing itself. My ex stood next to a door, his eyes shining. I couldn't tell with what.

"She's well," Dr. Z said, "and really, isn't that all you can ask for?" He looked like he might pounce. He looked uncomfortable in his clothes, like maybe he wished to take them off and bask in the sun.

These days, my ex and I remember the moment differently. He smiles and talks about how love is love, how good parenting means unconditional acceptance. He's forgotten the feeling of sinking, loss like a stone dragging us down.

The fear of knowing that no matter who our daughter was, someday she'd fly.

Dr. Zulaski looked at me with his golden eyes for a very long time.

YOUR SICK

We said *In sickness and in health*, and the state made it legal. I wore yellow and you wore blue. Together we shimmered between *hunter* and *emerald*. We hired a DJ. Guests slept on the floor.

We were one of the first of our kind to divorce: my lips pursed, your fingernails sharp. I deleted your email, your number, your ring. Our friends were angry, as if we'd done it to them.

A few years later we met at a conference. I was on business; you ran the hotel. You discounted my stay, sent a bottle of wine. You were generous and cheerful and used my full name.

That night the phone rang while I was taking a shower. We talked about rain, what we missed about thunder. Later that night you knocked on my door. We didn't mention our invisible *We*.

After the conference, I called and texted but you didn't answer. A few months later I worked up the nerve to visit the hotel, a day's drive away in a minor city.

Don't forget she took you to court.

But I'd forgotten everything except the taste of your mouth, the way you walked, and the way you stood still.

When I got to the hotel I tried to page you. I repeated your name over and over. No one at the hotel had ever heard of you. I paced the lobby, trying to decide what to do. I chose dinner in the hotel restaurant. The waiter sat me near the kitchen, which bothered me until I realized I could see everyone in the room: suits and soldiers, families and prostitutes. At first I didn't notice you in a chair by the window. Lipstick, and you'd dyed your hair. You were talking to a very beautiful woman. The wine was the wine you'd sent to my room.

I finished my dinner. As I left the restaurant I dropped my check on your table and smiled at your date. You wore a nametag, but it wasn't your name. You looked up at me and your eyes glazed with panic.

Later that night you knocked on my door. Just to be sure it was you I called out your old name and your new name, both.

It's me, you said. I wasn't sure which *me* you meant, which name to use, but it didn't matter. You ran your fingers through my hair. You pressed me up against the sink and things happened that weren't supposed to happen, now that we weren't together.

You had the key to every room.

In one of those rooms you made me sick.

Sickness slid from lips to cheek, hairline to hipbone, bruise to nick.

Your sickness swam the skeins of my blood, but I didn't know. I didn't know anything.

Your new name was Yetta. Your old name also began with Y, but I was beginning to wonder if your old name was fake. Were you Yetta, Yelena, or Yumi? Yvonne or Yolanda? Ysolde or Yael?

I stayed in the hotel for a week. Every morning you

slipped me a key and every evening you looked slightly different. You walked into the room and in five seconds flat we were on the bed. I made you remove the comforter. *No offense*, I said. *I'm sure it's clean.* I didn't call out your name during sex. I praised your piercings, your Falstaff tattoo.

Finally I asked about *Yetta.*

On casual Fridays we change our names to whatever.

I rolled you over and straddled you and pinned your hands to the headboard. *Tell me the truth.*

The truth about what?

Anything.

Anything?

Something.

I'm sick.

I unpinned your hands.

It's contagious.

You're kidding.

This isn't a joke. Don't you want to know what I gave you?

I went into the bathroom and locked the door.

You turned on the TV. I could hear conservative pundits and the shopping channel. I flooded the shower, bathtub, and sink.

When I opened the door you were gone.

It took me a while to notice the note taped to the phone:

> *Dear Emily,*
>
> *Please don't contact me again. I've moved on and so should you. I thought you could handle something casual but clearly you're still an emotional vortex. Also I'm sorry I made you sick, but it's not that bad. You might even like it.*
>
> *Ex,*
>
> *Y*

I read the note several times. Then I lay on the bed and scanned my body, like in yoga class, except I was looking for traces of you. Whatever you left behind in me. The microchip, the shard of stained glass you slid behind my knee or into the crook of my arm. Marks like a spider bite, the venom already in my bloodstream.

What is it? I said to the empty room. *Where is it?*

I put a hand over my throat, felt for the pulse. My fingers found it—*thump, thump*—and it stopped. I pressed harder. Minutes passed and then, just as abruptly, the thumping returned. Water spilled over the side of the bathroom sink and soaked the carpet. Someone knocked on my door.

You might even like it.

Something casual.

I've moved on.

An ache welled in my throat like tears, just below the pulse I'd felt stop and restart. My skin came alive. The room rolled. *Thump, thump,* and I was out the hotel door, into the city, your city, carrying some invisible piece of you.

You were inside me in some crucial way, and the you in me made me do things. I bought baseball hats. Vodka. I slipped into your accent, borrowed your syntax. I lost weight, ground my teeth. I even phoned your mom, once, just to hear her voice, and she called out a name that wasn't yours and wasn't mine. *Eleanor?* she said, and I said, *Yes*, and she said, *I told you not to contact me here.* We were all other people, acting out lives as if we owned them.

I cut my hair, affected a swagger, laughed loudly at things that weren't jokes. The sickness in me spread. I introduced myself as Eleanor, gave your hometown as my own, developed a taste for raw oysters. As you, I became a regular at bars I'd never gone to, and I used facts about serial killers to hit on women. As you, I never went home alone.

I didn't tell the women I slept with that I was sick. They wouldn't understand until they went to the doctor, maybe, complaining that they didn't feel like themselves.

It's an illness, the doctors would tell them. *You're not yourself.*

They were me.

And I was you.

And you were someone else.

We were all shifting places, pretending we didn't see ourselves walking down the street.

I married one of these women. I told her my name was Edith. Hers, Yaris. She could've been you, far gone. I was far gone, too, but something in her mouth reminded me of the old me, and you the old you. When I told her I was sick, she said she was, too. We didn't know what that meant, and by that point we didn't care. We traded *my place or yours* for hotel rooms, one after the other, where I ran my fingers through her hair, pushed her up against the sink. She touched my lips and told me words she wanted me to say: *broom* and *handbag* and *skillet.* She fell in love after our third date, third room. I felt how different it was to be in love as you, how distant. I finally understood you better. I thought Yaris was close enough. *Marry me,* I said, her fingers in my mouth.

I'd like to say we found each other again, one sickness a cure for the other, and that Yaris became you and I became me. It happens; you hear stories of people who find each other again a year later, fifteen years, fifty. I wish I could say we'd changed enough to make us fit again. But it wasn't like that. Yaris turned picky and dull, and I left her in a hotel room, locked in the bathroom, faucets gushing.

Dear You, I wrote, *This isn't working. I'm sorry.*

Restrained myself from, *It isn't you, it's me.*

I walked out of that hotel feeling free. Did it matter that

it was just the next phase of the sickness if it felt like being cured? It was enough that I no longer waited for your call. No longer looked for you in crowds. I no longer saw couples that looked like you and me—maybe they were you and me—and felt sick about their luck.

STRUCK

Every girl's been struck but me. Lightning has taken more from my family than any war. It's taken pigment and nails and IQ. Memories. Platelets. Gave my aunt hepatitis, caused my cousin's stillbirth. Cured my sister Lanie of diabetes and ever getting cold. She glows now. Slightly, so you wouldn't notice unless you knew her from before.

My time is coming. No one knows why it's only the girls who get struck, but it doesn't matter why because that's how it is. You can't escape it. They say it hurts but it's over fast. Afterward anything can happen. If your heart stops, you better hope someone nearby knows CPR and isn't afraid to touch you. Lanie's heart didn't stop, but she was paralyzed for two weeks after, and she said she smelled fire the whole time. She communicated by blinking, but all she'd tell us was that something was burning. Her hair was singed off, so that made sense. But she also said she kept thinking of this phrase, *Get her out of the water*, and she didn't know why. Didn't know who said it or where she'd heard it. She thinks it was some kind of premonition, and that it has something to do with me.

People who've been struck are always talking about their premonitions. After hers, my mom developed reverse ESP, where after everything that happened, she said, *I knew that was going to happen.*

Lanie thinks I should go swimming. Storm swimming. She doesn't like that I've been left behind. She's only ten months older than me. We could've been bio sisters. Mom had been on the adoption waiting list so long that a surprise pregnancy didn't deter her, so she got us both. Lanie and I have always been close. She tells Mom she's going to help me so that I don't become one of those people like our great-grandma, who didn't get struck until she was eighty-three. She had to wait her whole life, and then she died from it so she didn't even get to enjoy it. Mom tells Lanie to be patient, that it's not a competition. Moms have to say those kinds of things, even though really, with us girls, everything's a competition. Lanie goes around in her sports bra and shorts, skin tinged red like she's been in the sun, and she starts sentences with *When I was struck*, and every time she says it, it's like she's won something.

The next time I hear thunder in the distance, I tell Mom I'm going on a walk. She nods and tells me to be safe. Lanie high-fives me on the way out.

"This is your day," she says. "I can feel it."

"How do you know?" I say.

She pauses, thinking. Her face perpetually flushed. "I just do," she says. "Look." She holds out an arm covered in tiny bumps. "A chill. I didn't even feel it."

"What will happen to me?" I say.

She shrugs. "Maybe you'll be able to breathe underwater. Maybe your eyes will change color." She levels a gaze at me. "Maybe your problem will go away."

"Yes," I say. "Maybe."

My problem was that I kept trying to get people to dare me to kiss girls. It was funny at first. Then it stopped being funny.

At school they called me Lightning Girl because they knew I was waiting to get struck. *Why don't you just stick your finger in a socket?* they said. *Why don't you take a bath with a hair dryer?*

I could if I wanted to, I said. *I could hold a live wire. I could kiss Jenny Miller. Dare me.*

We don't want to dare that anymore, they said. *We want*

you to lick a battery.

If you dare me to kiss her, I'll do it, I said. *You'll see.*

You're boring, they said. *We'd rather watch television.*

And they would all leave, and Jenny Miller or whoever would stick out her tongue at me, and I'd be alone on the playground.

I thought maybe after I was struck I wouldn't care so much about being alone. There were kids who were like that naturally, and it seemed they had this advantage. I hoped my gift from being struck was at least something useful, like never having to be cold.

Lanie was lucky. She already knew exactly who she was. She had a ride to Cloud Lake every Saturday night. College kids hung out at the lake on weekends, a place to park and a place to swim. Beer in bottles and pills from a doctor. Skinny dipping and diving from the highest ledge. I knew these things because Lanie told me. Like lightning, she'd gone fast and first. I wanted to ride, but she wouldn't let me. "After you've been struck," she'd say.

The next time I see storms in the distance, I tell Mom I'm going on a walk. Lanie high-fives me on the way out, but she's wrong this time; all I'm after is the rain. The bus waits at the stop, and a creep offers me a ride, but I walk for an hour, all the way to Goodwill. My babysitting money buys a swimsuit and a necklace: a silver chain with an *L* for *Love.*

L is for Lanie, who thanks me when I give her the necklace, wrapped in tissue I found in Mom's drawer. "It's perfect," she says, hooking the clasp. "*L* is for lightning."

L is for lure.

I watch her watch herself in the mirror, smiling at her face on fire.

"CanIgotothelakewithyou?"

Lanie sighs, hot pink. "Just don't dive in the shallows. I

don't want to play lifeguard if you break your neck."

Saturday night takes forever to happen. After basketball practice Lanie dawdles in the shower and uses all the hot water. She comes into our bedroom and sits on the floor.

"I'm so glad my hair grew back," she says. Sometimes, when someone burns inside, their hair stays gone. Lanie got lucky. Her hair grew back curly, darker and thicker. "We're like birth sisters now."

I take my turn in the shower to hide how she's hurt me. Sometimes I worry that being adopted means I'll never be struck. While I'm washing my adopted hair and shaving my adopted legs, Lanie knocks on the door. Says she's sorry by showing me her tattoo: a lightning bolt. Mom doesn't know. "You should get one, too, because you're my sister. My real sister."

I drink it all down.

Then it's Saturday night, and someone's driving us somewhere in his lightning bolt car. I'm in the backseat, watching Lanie nod at MattMichaelMartin. His name keeps changing. Lanie looks over her shoulder and sticks out her tongue.

Cloud Lake is rock ledges circling a sheet of green glass. Mitchell grabs Lanie's hair like she might run away. I'm just watching from the backseat, invisible. When he tears off her shirt, I get out of the car.

I walk to the ledge and look out at the water, ripples in circles toward a faraway shore. There's a girl swimming backstroke near the broken pier. She's watching the sky, then the girl on the ledge.

The girl on the ledge is me.

The swimmer waves and I wave back. I want to kiss her and I want to be struck. Lanie stumbles out of the car, shirt on backwards, smiling a locked diary smile.

Clouds start raining. Then lightning, and the lake's on fire.

"Get her out of the water," someone screams.

I dive, which I don't know how to do. When I hit the

water, I know I've been struck. My body twitches and I fight to keep breathing. All I can see is broken green.

My swimmer's drowning, but she'd like to be saved.

"Hold on," I say. I put my arm across her chest and swim us both to the broken pier. Inside the water we're electric. The lake sizzles around us, kiss. I know people die this way, but I'm Lightning Girl, and I burn through water. My arms around her, she thrives on shock: it locks us together. When we clamber to shore, we're ordinary girls, bright zig-zag hidden inside us.

STORM SICK

The storm started inside me. My stomach swirled, a seasick funnel. Like carrying a tornado, fat with barn doors and flying cattle. I was down to nonfat yogurt and apple slices, though I'd stopped being hungry months ago. In Algebra, numbers blurred above the board in clouds of chalk. I walked around in a fog-turned-twister. Not eating was hard until it was easy, so easy I didn't know who else to be.

I was in Homeroom when the storm touched down. Amber Alert sat in front of me, texting her boyfriend. My "B" for "Baxter" had followed her surname all the way to Pinecone High. While she tapped out abbreviations for words she didn't know how to spell, the storm inside me tripled its territory. No one noticed. Like when Kaitlyn got pregnant and our teachers ignored it until she went to the bathroom and came out with Briane.

Kaitlyn got expelled and Briane got adopted. I wondered what would happen to me once Pinecone realized the storm was my fault, a tornado fueled by hunger. By sophomore year, all the girls were skinny, but I amped it up because that's how I am. My Not Boyfriend called me intense. Said not eating was sexy. Said I looked like a boy. Sometimes I wondered about the sexy boy comment. But he wasn't my boyfriend, just some guy at the bank.

Not eating started while I was at camp. I lost weight on accident and liked how I looked. So instead of eating, I tried not eating. It was the same, sort of. All about food.

I thought Not Boyfriend would notice that I didn't have boobs, but he said I looked good and kept kissing my ear. He probably liked me because I was cheap. No dinner, no movie, just sex in his car.

The only person who noticed was Amber. She cornered me in the bathroom while I was brushing my teeth.

"Are you throwing up or just not eating?" Not out of concern, just wanting the facts.

"Not eating."

"Like Tina and Kimmy."

"Kind of," I said, "but they throw up, too."

My parents put me in therapy. Sort of a daycare, sandbox and dolls. The therapist had this tray full of sand and wanted me to draw pictures with crayons.

Cindi wore heels with tight jeans. "If you were an animal, what would you be?"

I tried to think of an animal that didn't eat, had anal sex with an old guy in his car on odd-numbered weeknights, and liked to read young adult novels about Girls Gone Wrong.

"I would be an echidna? Or a pangolin? Maybe a mouse?"

"Pick one." Her wedding ring was as thick as a nut.

After a few sessions playing with sand, moving furniture around in a dollhouse, and naming animals, she gave me a list of rules about eating:

Keep a food journal.

Eat three meals a day.

Meals must be spaced at least four hours apart.

Meals must include three different colored foods.

Finish all the food on your plate but do not eat more than one serving of each food.

Do not eat between meals.

Do not eat standing up.

Do not talk about stressful events while eating.

Share food with your family family-style.

Do not eat alone.

Do not keep food in your bedroom or in your personal belongings.

Weigh all unpackaged foods; record weight and size in your food journal.

Record your mood while eating: for example, happy or sad.

"Some of these are for girls who throw up. Like keeping food in your bedroom. That's a hoarding thing."

"How does that make you feel?"

"How does what make me feel?"

"What you just said."

"I just said a couple different things, though. I said some of these rules are for girls who..."

"It looks like our time is up for today. In our next session we'll discuss how you're adjusting to these rules. These are rules for life. You'll want to follow these rules for the duration."

The duration of what?

My parents asked how it went.

"Because she came highly recommended," Mom said to Dad. "The Haskells used her when Bettina went through a phase."

"Expensive. But anything you need." My dad ruffled my hair. "That's a good girl."

"We're supposed to eat dinner family-style." It sounded dirty. "That's what Cindi said."

"Shouldn't you call her Mrs. Donovan?"

"She said Cindi when I shook her hand."

"I don't know about first names in this instance."

"It seems too casual. Aren't they supposed to set firm boundaries?" Dad picked up his briefcase. "I need to get back to the office."

Mom turned away. "Another dinner meeting? That's the second this week."

I went into my room. Took out cleaning solution and paper towels and cleaned my desk. It had cat hair on it, and ink smears from homework. I taped the list of food rules over my bed. Duration. I didn't know what she meant. For the rest of my life or the rest of my sick?

Online the Pro-Ana girls were still skinnier than me. I stared at pictures of models until I found one who seemed to be staring back. She had cat's eye mascara and long legs. She was wearing a see-through white blouse, ribs like birds. Her name was probably Vetruska or Pommaline.

My cell vibrated in my pocket: Not Boyfriend.

"Come over," he said.

"Pick me up in fifteen."

In young adult novels, girls always climb out their windows, but I just walked out the door. "Bye Mom," I said, and she went back to cleaning. She vacuumed whenever my dad went out to wherever he went: often, who knows. Not Boyfriend, whose name was Brodie, sat in his car at the corner of Harrison and North.

"Good work," he said. "I'm your getaway car."

"Where to?"

"Your choice."

I tried to think of a place to park that we hadn't used in a while. Brodie was obsessed with changing places. Said cops might mistake him for a rapist and he could get arrested and it would be my fault if he went to jail. He said we had to be careful because my age hadn't caught up with my personality. That I didn't act fifteen, so I wasn't, really. He said I was hot and had a great ass. "Turn over," he'd say, and I'd lie on my stomach in the backseat. He had to get out of the car to get on top of me. Once, when it was cold outside, we tried staying in the car. That didn't work very well.

"Sunset Hill," I said. My favorite. Or used to be, when I went there with Amber. We were friends, best friends, until 9th grade. Then she got popular and I got sick.

Around midnight Brodie dropped me off a few blocks away from my house. Dad's car was still gone. Mom had put my dinner away in the fridge. No light under her door, but the

TV was still on. I took dinner out and unwrapped it. There was a note on top: For Ana Love Mom. It was baked chicken, broccoli, apple slices, and a whole wheat roll. I took out the food scale and weighed the chicken, broccoli, and apple slices. I wasn't sure if I should weigh the roll. My legs swayed, and the kitchen lights clouded. The stirring inside me funneled into a storm.

I was in the bedroom, dozing to the TV, when I heard the crash. Everything went dark. I hurried in the direction of the kitchen, feeling along the walls for the light switch. Flipped it to nothing. No power. "Ana?" Nothing. A sound like static. "Are you okay?" My eyes wouldn't adjust fast enough. Shapes of refrigerator and faucet. Ana on her feet by the counter. I kicked broken glass before I got to her. Reached down and touched cold broccoli. "Are you okay?"

"I feel funny."

"What happened?"

"I don't know. I dropped my plate."

Feeling for the drawer with the matches and candles. The strange static noise getting louder.

"What's that hissing?"

"I don't know. But Mom?" Found match, struck match, and finally I could see her. Head bent, hair hanging. "I think it's coming from me."

In the candlelight, her pupils swam. I brought the light closer. I can't describe it – they churned. They blew around in her eyes. Then I noticed her hair puffing back from her face. Slightly, but there it was. She was caught in a wind I couldn't feel. Not caught in it; she was it. Looking at her made me dizzy.

"Ana, take my hand."

"I don't want to scare you, but I'm having trouble seeing."

"I'm not scared," I said, though I was.

Then she bent at the waist and vomited wind. It howled out of her and rattled the front door.

I took her hand. With the other hand, I texted her dad because whatever was happening, I wanted it to happen on his turf. He was better in emergencies. He was better with Ana. But he didn't answer, so I led Ana to the front door. She moved carefully, like she was in danger of falling. Or breaking. I put an arm around her waist, and immediately understood two things. There was nothing between my hand and Ana's bones; and whatever was in her eyes was in her skeleton, too. Her ribcage rumbled like train tracks. It crackled with electricity.

"Shit," I said, trying to hurry her along. She wouldn't be hurried. My fingers gripped into her bones, and her bones softened in response. I felt the give and pulled tighter. I couldn't get her to move.

She was so easy to lift. Like a bird, like a cage. Her ribs were buoyant. Better than weightless. It pushed her up, away, and I lost my grip. Her whole face was swirling. All but unrecognizable. She floated, and I jumped for her. Caught a thrumming anklebone before it disappeared. Clutched the mess of her to my chest and ran for the car.

I felt her voice in my ear: I need to eat.

I knew we were not going to make it to the car.

Illness has a way of taking hostages. She was my daughter, so my job, since before she was born, was to feed her.

She wrested free of me in the middle of the driveway. Swirled around, all that suppressed hunger and attenuated life rushing free. A funnel, body temperature, that snaked around my legs. She'd already begun collecting sticks and gravel.

You throw your baby to the world, to the wolves, and sometimes they bring the world back. The gravel drew blood.

"Stop it!" I shouted. "You're acting like a spoiled child!"

A car drove by, passengers pointing. I felt ridiculous. She wasn't acting like a child at all. She was acting like a storm because she was a storm. A funnel cloud, specifically, ringing and spitting debris. I waited a few minutes to see if she would end, or become herself again, or dissipate. She waited too, and when she ejected rocks, they no longer seemed aimed at me.

I wondered if this was about punishment or revenge or drama. Somehow the funnel cloud had gangly teenage appendages. She seemed embarrassed about her outburst. She seemed hungry. She seemed to be listening to the sky. Then I was listening to the sky, too. A whine, like bees. Then louder, and she was gone.

Texts from my husband flashed on my phone. Don't panic and I'm on my way and Tornado sirens. You ok? And Roads shut down. Power out. And Dear god, Pinecone hit.

Ana was the first, but not the only. They did just what you'd imagine teenagers-turned-storms might do. After they leveled the high schools, they raided the mall. They targeted bullies and ex-boyfriends. They overturned convertibles, cleaned out banks. They opened cages at the dog pound and the zoo. They issued lists of rules for their families:

Do not tell us what to do.

Do not try to stop us.

Do not give us lists of rules.

Do not tell us how you feel: for example, disappointed, worried, upset.

Be sure to record your valuables for the insurance company.

Some parents left town, others started a support group. My husband joined, and he brought in physicians and psychiatrists as guest speakers. The support group members spoke of their daughters in past tense, their storms in present. They talked about their disappointment, their worry. They bemoaned their storms' recklessness, and greed, and invincibility.

Sometimes when my husband told me about these meetings, he couldn't help a bit of pride from edging into his voice.

One destroyed a 7-Eleven.

One a monster truck rally.

One a Catholic church.

One a motel.

Ana was my daughter; I can say that now. I don't know exactly when it happened, the shift from is to was, but now it's done. Sometimes I don't see her for weeks; sometimes I only hear of her on the news. I try not to feel guilty. I try to observe without judgment. She calls my husband more than me, and when I hear him talking to her, I try not to listen. I don't ask if there have been any changes. I don't ask what she's eaten.

THE STORM GROWER

The garden is in the backyard. Hurricane, tornado, blizzard. Betty grows them in rows, strung up on the fence with twine. Neighbors come to her with their demands, and she gives them shoots and cuttings and bulbs: a hurricane eye in a Styrofoam cup. "Keep it moist," she tells them, or, "Plenty of light." They walk from her house carefully, down the front porch steps cradling weather. They use the storms for insurance claims, to get rid of unsightly properties, to deal with termite problems or annoying neighbors. "Watch the size on this one," she says of a super cell in a glass dome. "Could get out of control."

They come to her with needs and cash, and she sends them away with solutions.

One day a child rings the bell. He has longish hair, brownish eyes. A ball cap cocked to the side. He shifts from foot to foot and tries to look into her house, calls her Missus, offers to cut the grass. Rusty mower on the sidewalk behind him. He does a terrible job, zigzagging across the yard, leaving unmowed patches sticking up like cowlicks, and she realizes she's forgotten to ask what he charges. She gets out the checkbook, and he shifts again from foot to foot. "Do you got like a thunderstorm or something?" he says without looking at her.

"And what do you need with a thunderstorm?" Betty waits while he tries not to answer.

"I'm not as huge as some of them," he says, becoming smaller as he says it. She doesn't know how old he is supposed to be. She would guess fifth grade, and she remembers that fifth grade is when kids begin to grow at different rates, like in July when cold fronts wilt while monsoons bloom.

"Maybe something small," she says and leaves him on the porch. A bit of low pressure, she thinks, enough to cause short but heavy rain on a hot day. Something he can use to impress his friends. She is dividing up a leggy section when she hears the screen door click shut. The clippings fall from her hands. The boy is in the yard, yanking a whole tornado out by the roots. She hears the thick tubers snapping. The boy falls backwards with the effort, but he is up again before she can get to him – the arthritis in her knees – and running away. "Please, don't," she shouts after him. He leaves his mower and the wrecked lawn behind.

The destruction is predictable and immediate. A trailer park wiped out, seven people critically injured, two daring rescues, half a dozen heroic pets. The information comes to Betty in a myriad of ways. People eye her backyard, purse their lips. Already she's had the cops called on her twice, but she produces all the necessary permits and they go away. When they come this time, she shrugs. "Not my doing," she says, and they go away.

That night Betty lays awake listening to radio reports in the dark. She needs better security, she thinks. The next day, she buys floodlights and a guard dog that barks whenever someone comes near her front porch.

So it is strange when she goes to check the mail, dog asleep in his crate, and there's another child at her door, this one a girl in a brown dress. "Now what on earth," Betty says, but the girl is visibly shaking so Betty lets her in, gives her a cup of herbal tea. She waits for the girl to offer her story. "I just want him to stop," the girl says, and it's all she really needs to say, the rest filled in by her downcast eyes, her nervous hands.

"Okay." Betty holds up a hand. "I can give you something."

In the garden, the child loses herself for a moment, darting among the rows. The heat waves are in full bloom, straining their wire cages. The droughts need staked. Even the ice storms are beginning to bud, volunteer storms from the ones she'd let go to seed last year.

The girl examines the storms, chooses carefully. Lands on a plot at the back, a shady spot where not much else will grow. "I think this will do," she says. She points to an earthquake, an exotic. It's a flamboyant, dangerous choice. Everyone will know where it came from.

"That one's not ready to be picked," she says, and the girl gives her a long look. Betty deftly twists off a couple pods of heat lightning, drops them in a rubber bowl. "This should work."

The girl accepts the offering. Still, Betty leaves the gate unlocked that night, just in case. She's not at all surprised to find the earthquake gone by morning.

That day, a whole suburb is leveled. People who never thought to earthquake-proof their homes are crushed by falling bookcases, cabinets, roofs. Tremors are felt in cities across the state.

When the police come to Betty's door, she speaks to them from behind the screen door, holding the dog by the collar. "I had nothing to do with it," she says, "and that's all I'll say." From an upstairs window, she watches them circle her house, test the back gate, try to peer over the fence. They leave, but she knows they'll be back.

Weeks later, Betty wakes to crying: animal-reckless, pitched too high. She expects a coyote pup stuck in the fence or a pregnant rabbit. Instead a plastic laundry basket filled with dirty laundry and a wailing baby.

Pinned to the baby's chest: BAD BABY.

Pinned to the laundry: WASH 'N DRY.

Betty leaves the basket beside a row of flood saplings. Pressed to her chest, the child's crying stops. She thinks of the children she might've chosen, the husband who never came back from the war.

Baby curls its fists, unclenches. The candles on the sill catch fire.

That night she sleeps with her dog at the foot of the bed, baby in a makeshift crib. Dog and baby snore in sync. In the morning she knows she needs to name them. So many storms in her book of designs.

She names her dog Thunder and her baby Lightning, but calls them both Chester. When the police knock a week later, looking for a misplaced baby, a bad baby full of fire and dirty laundry, she has no idea what they're talking about. And this is her nephew, Chester. And Chester's a good baby and a very clean dog.

Chester grows. Chester learns to gesture. Chester barks and Chester sends tiny shoots of lightning from his wrinkled fists.

Betty's busy with storm season, which lasts all year. She struggles to make ends meet. Tries two-for-one hailstorms and discount downpours. Wonders if she should go back to school, try an online program in equine massage.

One morning she's feeding Chester, spooning butternut squash puree into his mouth, when Chester starts barking. A tall man rings the bell. He has close-cropped hair and angry eyes. A ball cap cocked to the side. He shifts from foot to foot and tries to look into her house. Tsunami, she thinks. Flotsam, no jetsam.

"Your kid put a curse on my monster truck."

From inside the house, flickers of light like knots in a storm.

"Nonsense," says Betty, but before she can shut the door,

he's barged inside. The angry man stands in the center of Betty's knick-knacks, on her pastel shag carpet, in front of her television, and points at her son.

"That's him. That's the kid who cursed me. Every time I drive by your house, my truck breaks down."

"You watch too much TV."

"That kid's possessed."

"I don't believe in the devil."

"Aren't you the storm grower? Devil's work if there ever was."

Now Chester's howling, the way he howls at sirens, the way a lost child howls for its mother. Lightning strikes. The man was right. Post-sizzle, he's embers on her princess plush rug.

In the morning, Betty spreads ash on her garden. Slugs and snails play keep away. This time she remembers to avoid the potatoes. Sprinkles small blizzards with soft gray snow.

CARDIAC PARASITE

I found it in a well. Small and water-logged, limp, muddy-eyed. It didn't actually have eyes. But it had this expression like a drowning hamster, two bulges on either side of what seemed to be a head, a sour shape for a mouth. I pulled up the bucket and it was draped over the edge, and when I put out my hand, it sort of collapsed onto me, pulling warmth from my palm. It purred. I took it home.

"What on earth?" my mom said. She was used to me bringing home wild animals to tame, strays, kids without families. My room was full of handmade litter boxes, rope leashes, cardboard kennels. Sloughed-off skins and extra toothbrushes, the press-on nails Kaitlyn Carver left in my trashcan after she spent the night. I keep the fingernails in my nightstand to remind me that she was really here.

"I'm not sure what it is," I said. "It was in the well." As it dried, its black spine showed.

Mom took off her glasses and looked closer. "Some kind of reptile?"

"I don't think so. It was in bad shape when I found it. Looks better now." It'd straightened up some, was sort of sniffing around. It didn't exactly have a nose. It moved its head from my shoulder to mom's hands to a kitchen chair. Already I noticed it could mimic certain facial expressions. At the moment, it looked hopeful.

"It is kind of cute." Mom held out her hand for it to smell or lick, and it did both, sort of, and also neither. Then it sneezed and left grey-black goo on her wrist. "Friendly."

I waited for Mom to remember herself, and in a minute she did. "Just a couple of days," she said, hands on hips. "And no begging to keep it. As soon as it's better it goes right back to where it belongs. It looks like a baby whatever-it-is, and who knows what it'll be like when it gets bigger."

I nodded, and the thing waved its head around.

"I don't want another infestation," she said. For a while I'd brought home things that bred faster than I could keep up with, and the house was overrun with mice in the walls and moths in the closets and opossums in the attic, and even Kaitlyn said she'd gotten knocked up because of me, even though I told her that what we did wasn't procreative. She said no but maybe whatever was wrong with me was contagious, and maybe I'd gotten it from all those animals I kept around. But the mice shredded all the toilet paper, and the moths ate holes in the curtains, and the opossums mated with their own children and spent the night hissing and clomping around over our heads. Mom said it was a health hazard and called an exterminator. She worried I was trying to mad scientist things. I called her Hitler. The opossums were carted out in death bags. None of us wanted a repeat.

And Kaitlyn still ate lunch with me, but she didn't come over anymore.

"Just a few days," I said, though of course I had no intention of setting it free.

The thing shook its head at me so Mom didn't have to. She was the opposite of a packrat, always conducting clean sweeps and going to detox diets. When Kaitlyn was over, Mom kept offering her veggie sticks. "I think your mom thinks I'm fat," Kaitlyn had said.

"That's just how she flirts," I said.

"Gross."

That was my problem. I made jokes no one laughed at, and later, even I couldn't understand why I'd thought they were funny. It was like I kept becoming different people with the same problem.

Mom looked from me to the thing and back to me.

"Whatever happened to Kaitlyn? She seemed so nice."

I looked at the thing, too. It leapt from my hand and scurried or rolled under the table. Sort of hovered on the floor, barely touching its feet down. It didn't really have feet.

"I don't know," I said. "She got struck by lightning or something."

"Good lord."

"It made her famous." I kneeled and held out my hands. The thing crept or glided back immediately. I'd first thought I'd keep it in a bucket of water with a few rocks. Now I decided on a box and blanket next to my bed.

My mom touched my face. "How did she take to her new fame?"

"Like a champ." I didn't tell Mom about Kaitlyn's fake pregnancy because I didn't want her to interfere.

"You going to name it?" my mom said. I named all of my animals after holidays.

"Yeah. I think Columbus."

"As in, the day? Or the city?"

"The Spaniard," I said.

She smiled, and the thing sort of smiled back at her. They were already bonding, and there was no way Mom was going to make me get rid of it. Which made me realize that maybe, if I showed my new pet to Kaitlyn, it'd help me keep her, too.

One of my brothers poked his head in my room while I was getting Columbus settled in. "What the crap is that?" he said.

"An enlarged amoeba," I said. "Maybe a shrunken mole." It's important to be direct with boys, so I felt pressure to be sure.

"Looks like one of those things," he said.

"What things?"

"You know." He put a hand over his chest, pledge-of-allegiance-style. "That eat your heart."

"This isn't one of those. And they don't eat your heart."

He meant the rumors at school about why so many kids were getting sick. Something was sucking the life out of them, and some blamed a parasite in the drinking water that wormed its way through the bloodstream to the heart. I figured that if teenagers wanted to say they were heartsick, it was probably true one way or another.

If Kaitlyn says I got her pregnant, I could say that she gave me a parasite.

But I won't say that because I found Columbus in a well.

The next day at lunch Kaitlyn sat next to me and unwrapped the smelliest sandwich.

"I have to eat protein because I'm pregnant."

"You're so not pregnant."

"What's in your lap?"

Columbus sat swaddled in wool, snoring against my belly. I'd snuck to school in a giant sweater.

"You look like a cutter with those crazy long sleeves."

"I'm babysitting a ferret." I uncovered Columbus's tiny sort of face. It sneezed.

"Oh my God! Love!"

Columbus squeaked. Squirmed in Kaitlyn's direction.

"Boy ferret or girl?"

"Other, I guess. Its name is Columbus. It's not really a ferret."

Kaitlyn talked to Columbus in a sugary voice. Columbus went crazy, nipping my arm. Crawled down my elbow out the cuff of my sweater. Made a beeline for Kaitlyn, squeaking.

"It's totally a kitten."

"Kaitlyn, I know what a kitten looks like."

"It needs a mom or a sister or something. Can I keep it?

Please?"

Columbus was in love with Kaitlyn, making nuzzling sounds, licking her face.

"Okay. But I get visitation and stuff. Two weekends a month."

"Deal."

"And you have to stop saying I made you pregnant."

"What should I say, then?"

Columbus hummed. I took off my oversize rainbow stripe sweater and gave it to Kaitlyn. "Just say we're family."

Columbus sort of waved itself around in agreement, so Kaitlyn nodded.

Then History, where we learned about The War on Terror.

All day I had heart palpitations. I knew right where Kaitlyn parked her bike, and for a full three periods I allowed myself the montage: riding her handlebars, pushing Columbus on a swing at the park, the three of us walking hand-in-not-really-a-hand. I knew better than to indulge in this kind of thinking. I knew that the family I had was the one I had. Me and Mom and a mess of brothers.

I walked home from school a different way so I wouldn't have to see Kaitlyn riding her bike, Columbus strapped to the back in a tiny helmet. No way was I regressing to stuffed animals. But the opossums didn't want to be held and then my Mom killed them and moths were no fun. I walked for a long time, then realized I was lost. I'd turned down Jones Road, which was all pasture, and now I was surrounded by horses and cows and tractor parts and nothing that really looked like a road.

Some guy drove by in a pickup truck and waved. The sun was fierce overhead but I could tell it would get dark early. I was smart about the sky like that. I took my phone and texted Chad:

Yo bro Im lost

Lost where

If I knew Id be home

So figure it out

"Fuck you," I yelled at my phone, which had a picture of Columbus as a screensaver. Another pickup, a tractor, a horse. I sat down by a fence and ate a candy bar. Then I got lucky and spotted a well.

It was on someone's land, but far enough away from their house that I risked it. Took off running over the field, past four-leaf clover, horse shit, and weeds.

The bucket was on a metal pulley, like ours. I used all my weight to lift the cover, little muscle knots in my arms. Splattered dirt all over my jeans.

"Ugh," I grunted, like Chad lifting weights in the garage. The cover came off and I lowered the bucket.

It came up half-full, something shiny and white on the bottom.

BAD BABY

She's done what she's supposed to do: strung herbs from the nursery ceiling, lit candles and incense, recited what the sick book told her to. Still the baby gets worse. One day Barb found him covered in mucus thick like slime. Another, he bit her and left behind an air-filled sac that, when popped, emitted a putrid smell. The baby's parents can ignore this, but not Barb. She's the one with him all day. She's the one getting bit.

The parents have given her instructions that she follows, and every morning the mother tells her she thinks they're working. They're not working. The mother says, "Today will be a good day," and then she twists her hair into a bun and zips her purse and leaves with the father in a cloud of perfume. Then Barb breathes deeply, steadies her face, and heads up to the nursery. To little Ben, not quite a year old. Already his voice has changed; already he's growing facial hair; already he prefers cold meat to anything else. She's not sure what he's becoming, and if the parents know, they aren't telling. Some of these kids grow out of it. Some don't. Nearly all run away as soon as they can, and the woods are becoming populated with them. They have their own bars, their own ramshackle neighborhoods. Modified pirate flags tacked to front doors, red on black, crossbones uncrossed.

Ben's a decent kid for the most part, when he isn't setting things on fire. Barb can always find the good in people, which is why she's good at this job. There aren't many sitters who'll take on Bad Babies, so she's got her pick. She likes Ben because he's creative. Like today: when she gets up to the nursery it's frozen solid. A duller kid would've turned the room upside down or covered it in fog. But Ben's got verve. She doesn't know if the Bads have leaders, but if they do, Ben will have a decent shot at president when he grows up.

She slides across the frozen floor and surveys the damage. Ben's in his crib, looking like a normal baby under ice. She'll have to chip him out and wait for the thaw, which could take all morning. He'll be late for his nap, which means that when the mother returns midday, she'll be upset. "But this is our time," she'll tell Barb, and Barb will feel weak with regret.

Mothers of Bad Babies are always in need of release. Distraction. They know what's happening to their children, and they know they can't do anything about it, and they feel – they've confided to Barb before – like bad mothers. Barb reassures them. She holds them. And, when it seems right, Barb runs a hand up their shirts or down their skirts and helps them forget for a while.

Once, Ben's mother asked Barb if she ever wanted babies of her own. She didn't have the nerve to tell the truth about the babies she'd had. Plump twins. Both bad.

Sometimes Barb thinks she sees them, hovering on the edge of the forest that runs parallel to Main Street, perpendicular to Elm. Of course she can't be sure. Of course by now they might be any age, look like anyone's wild things. She didn't give them up for adoption or sell them for labor. She loved them. Didn't care how bad. How fast they grew, how gray and bearded. How cruel.

It was the twins who didn't love, or not enough to stay. She woke up one midnight tied to the bed, cold air blowing in from the window. It took hours to unloose their knots. Her cats sat watching from the sill, uninterested in biting through twine. Once she freed herself she raced to the crib.

Empty. And footprints in the flower bed outside, two tiny sets headed straight for the woods.

Barb slides back out of the nursery and searches for an ice pick. Ben can get himself out, if he wants to. But Bad Babies often enjoy being rescued, and Barb doesn't mind being the rescuer. She puts a cut of red meat on the counter, thinking hunger might speed up the thaw. The floorboards above her creak from the weight of the ice. Bad Babies habitually destroy houses. The parents are always worrying over money, but as long as the kid is sick, Barb knows her job is safe. The parents need her. She's the last expense to get cut.

She locates a knife and the mother's office number.

"Ben's going to have a late nap today. Wanted to let you know."

"Everything okay?"

"Nothing I can't handle."

Barb pictures the mother at work, feet on the desk, momentarily lulled by talking as if Ben's normal.

The mother drops her voice. "I miss you. When can we meet?"

"Oh, honey." The floorboards groan, and Barb glances up. The ceiling looks bowed. "Got to go," she says.

"Tonight? Can I see you tonight?"

Cindi's voice has an edge to it. Sometimes the mothers try to get Barb to run away with them, to start new lives. Sometimes Barb is tempted.

"Okay. Tonight."

She hangs up and heads upstairs.

That night Ben's parents arrive home to a flooded kitchen, their son gnawing on steak tartare, frostbite etched into his cheeks like Lichtenberg figures. They don't blame Barb, but they don't blame Ben, either. Barb goes home to check on her cats.

She's opening a can of alphabet soup when Cindi texts her.

Can I come over?

She's never asked to come over before. Barb looks around her studio apartment, miniature fridge and single bed covered in cat fur, and invents a roommate on the spot.

Cindi texts back: *John's passed out on the sofa. Meet me here?*

On my way.

Barb turns off the stove, eats an energy bar. Shakes cat food into the fish-shaped bowl. Decides to walk, since it's hardly dark and still high summer, night air thick and warm and blue.

She walks down Main Street, peering into windows where families sit feeding babies bad and good, where no one seems to sit alone. She's one of the few; even her neighbors are crammed two, three, four to a studio.

Beyond the lights of tight families, the woods.

The woods are pine, each tree perfect, symmetrically staggered in rows of dense green. Beyond pine, more pine. Then blinding sharp branches, then the unknown where bad babies must go.

Tonight Barb tries not to think about the missing. About the Amber Alert that echoed across the internet. About insinuations, always veiled, that she'd made the whole thing up. That she'd never had children. That her mind had gone missing, confusing cats with children, as if all feral creatures smelled the same to their mothers.

Tonight she focuses on Cindi; Cindi of the short skirts and ruffled blouses; nights of lace and nights of sighs. They've never been so bold as to rendezvous with John in the house. She's turned on by the thought of a thin, secret scrim.

At the corner of Main and Elm her phone vibrates: Cindi.

John woke up. Too risky. Tomorrow?

Barb slides her finger over the trash can icon.

Turns around. Thinks of mint chocolate chip ice cream stashed in the freezer. Walks faster. Thinks of her cats curled on either side of her knees while she sleeps. Smells pine, smells salt. Hear sirens far off, then closer a rattle. The rattle grows in rings like the rings of a tree.

She's close to her apartment building but the landmarks look blurry. Shop lights switch off like dominos until the street's dark blue and the rattling noise feels brighter than neon.

She's done what she's supposed to do. The forest glows with staghorn lichen. There's a name for this feeling. She steps toward an outline, toward that feral crepuscular.

X-RAY PINE

Winter at the office meant sick, not Santa, so I wasn't surprised when my cold wouldn't quit. I coughed into my sleeve, sucked lozenges through meetings. My pack-a-day habit had finally caught up.

One day Brian from Legal suggested Dr. Zulaski. Said the guy saved his daughter and his marriage, too. My cough felt worse, burning my throat. Michael made the call for me when my voice disappeared.

Zulaski had thick hands and a Cheshire grin, eyes framed by golden eyebrows and bushy hair. He made intense, piercing eye contact during the entire exam. My ex-wife would've loved the guy.

The doctor said: tumor.

The doctor said: cut.

I lay on the table and went under his knife.

When I came to, I was propped up in a hospital bed, gauzy with pain. A peppy nurse showed me how to click a button for meds. I clicked like crazy, floating and free.

Zulaski hovered over my bed, handsome face sculpted into concern. I waited for his perfect mouth to form the word cancer.

"X-rays tell stories based on the stories we tell them."

Fuck you. Do I have cancer or not?

"What we thought was a tumor was really a twig. Some people open their mouths wider than others when they breathe. Heroic Breathers, we like to call them. Occasionally they inhale seeds and grow flora in their lungs." He held up a cluster of pine needles. "This is your sick, Xavier. Your lungs grew into a tree. You'll be in pain until you heal from surgery, but otherwise you're perfectly healthy."

My chest hurt, a lightning strike scar where they'd cut to remove the tumor that wasn't. I clicked the button when he left the room.

Zulaski let me take my tree home in a latex glove half-filled with water. Michael insisted on planting it next to the porch.

"Maybe it'll grow and we can hang bird houses on the branches." Michael built bird houses lined with fake fur, but our manicured lawn had no trees and no birdsong. "Here's an article about Heroic Breathers. You're in fabulous company: da Vinci and Plath."

"I miss the gym."

"No gym for a month. Want me to whip up some oatmeal?"

"Vodka sounds fine."

That night I dreamed my tree was back, growing out of my chest, thick boughs decorated with ornaments. My skin healed seamlessly, without scarring or pain, but instead of hair, I had a head full of needles.

Michael and I woke up to someone pounding on our door.

"Curb your tree!"

Michael opened the door on a forest. Pine needles littered the porch; branches scratched the windows. The smell of pine was so strong it had color and shape.

"The neighborhood association will never allow it!" Mrs. Flannery and her husband wore matching plaid bathrobes. He held both coffee cups while she shook her fist.

Michael dealt with our favorite neighbors while I examined the tree splintering our porch. I touched bark, then pulled away. When I breathed, it pulsed. When it pulsed, it grew.

Our lawn hummed with birds.

Mrs. Flannery said something about a chainsaw.

"It's a nature preserve," I said. "Rare birds. Endangered. Eminent domain."

"I hear you, son." Mr. Flannery nodded. "When I was a boy, they took our farmland for highway. Barely paid us a thing, just paved overnight."

Mrs. Flannery looked skeptical. She made chopping motions with her hands.

"You boys tell your mother we said hello." The Flannerys had long ago decided we were brothers. When Agnes moved out and Michael moved in they created a narrative that made sense in their world. By the time we walked them off our property we'd agreed to join them for Sunday supper.

"Is supper lunch or dinner or both?"

"It's after church. I don't think the meal matters."

"Who can we call to chop down this tree?"

"My tree? It's breathing."

"It's growing, for sure."

"It's breathing."

"It's growing. Wait, what do you mean?"

I explained to Michael that I'd grown the tree in my lungs, that I had obligations now that it breathed on its own.

"Trees don't breathe."

"This one does."

"I love when you get all magical on me. It's so Radical Faeries."

"Don't tease."

We kissed.

"Seriously." Michael seemed taller than he'd been a minute ago. "I've never wanted to live in a forest."

"It'll keep out the neighbors."

"Clearly not."

"You'll get used to it." At that moment, a bird hit our big front window, the one that used to look out onto our treeless lawn.

"Oh!" Michael said. We could see where the bird had ricocheted. It lay motionless in the pine needles. "I don't like nature."

"It's just a bird." I didn't want to look too closely. It wasn't a songbird, but something bigger, colorful. "We'll put stickers on the window. It'll be like a lodge. A retreat."

"I can't even see the car," Michael said. "What if I get lost?"

"Don't talk to wolves."

"I'm serious."

"I'll leave a trail of bread crumbs."

He was upset, so I nodded—"I'll call someone, first thing"—and we left it at that. We agreed to a change of location, and Michael held my arm as we strolled through the wood, and in the car he admitted that the pine smelled better than an air freshener. We passed the Flannerys at work in their flower garden. They waved. "Sunday," I called out the window. Mrs. Flannery shouted something back that sounded like *Bring your wives.*

"What did she say?"

Michael shrugged.

"Can we get out of this?"

"You want to keep your tree," Michael said, "you have to play nice with the neighbors."

"Fifty bucks says they never come back."

Michael merged onto the highway, and the sky erupted into sunset. The skyline looked bigger—taller, glassier. It felt like my lungs were wooden. I opened my mouth, shallow inhalations. The air was smoke.

"You okay?"

"I can't breathe. I'm overthinking it."

"You're still healing."

The car hurtled past stands of pine, shopping plazas,

hotels. Everything erect as windpipes, all that recycled air. I opened my mouth wider. What if next I inhaled thistle or larva? What if metal shavings or insulation? Could I grow skyscrapers for Michael, turn my lungs into sites of production? I was no hero, and this was no fairy tale. I just needed to get well.

I counted breaths all the way to the restaurant, ate my food quickly, told Michael what he wanted to hear. Gave him the gift of a normal evening, hoping it wouldn't be our last. It was dark when we left the restaurant, and we fell silent in the car. It seemed like it took longer than usual to get home. "You owe me fifty bucks," Michael said when we pulled up.

The Flannerys stood on the curb, looking grim. The Mrs. had a plate of cookies; the Mr. had a flashlight.

"You boys have pets?" he said when we got out, and she added, "We heard noises."

"No pets."

The Mr. pointed the flashlight into the woods. "I was just about to go back for my shotgun."

"What kind of noises?" I said.

"Shrieking?" the Mrs. said.

Something swooped through the flashlight beam, and I saw a flash of red. "It's just birds."

"You can't possibly stay here," Mrs. Flannery said, drawing me back. "It looks dangerous. Your poor foundation."

"Of course we can. This is our home." I looked at Michael, who hadn't spoken. I wanted to know if he would go into the woods with me or not.

He checked his watch and shook his head.

"Come with us, then." Mrs. Flannery pulled my arm, stronger than she looked. The noises of the forest dimmed behind us, replaced by the *chuck chuck* of someone's sprinkler, the click of motion detector lights detecting. Driveways lit up in our wake, basketball hoops and begonias. I could feel Michael relax. I couldn't breathe.

"You'll stay the night with us," she said, "and we'll have

pancakes in the morning. I always wanted to own a B and B, didn't I?"

She had my arm in a vise grip. "Do you work out?" I said.

"Come on." She could've picked me up and carried me if she wanted to. Our shadows looked like we were holding hands, the plate of cookies jutting from me like a pregnant belly.

"Do you have children?" I said.

"I don't care for them."

"Me, neither. I like their books."

She slapped her leg. "Me too!"

"It's the happy endings."

"And the talking animals."

I was glad we'd found something in common. Michael and Mr. Flannery weren't helping the conversation, and silence made the air harder to breathe.

"It's how the bad guys are so easy to spot," I said.

Mrs. Flannery murmured assent. We walked up the Flannerys' driveway past their parked truck and r.v. to a big wooden door. Michael and I hadn't touched since the restaurant, so I took his hand.

"Welcome to Flannery Country," she said, throwing open the door. Inside the layout was a mirror image of our own, and everything else was a perfect opposite. The décor was taxidermy and cross-stitch. Hunting trophies stared slack-jawed on the walls. Framed bible verses sat on otherwise empty shelves.

I put my lips next to Michael's ear. "Ever feel like you're being watched?"

"Be polite."

"Why? Let's go home."

Mrs. Flannery led us down a hallway to a room with two single beds. There was an indentation in one of them, which she rushed to smooth out. "Make yourselves at home. You boys hungry? Do you like venison?"

"I should probably rest," I said, tapping my chest.

She nodded. "I'll leave you to it." After she left I said,

"You think she's happy?"

"How should I know?" Michael was shoving the two beds together. "Seems like they've been together forever."

"What if we can't go home?"

The beds lined up in the middle. Michael pulled a blanket over the seam. "What if we go home, and we can't get back out? That was supposed to be our starter home."

We got under the covers. The room was dark.

"I don't know if I can sleep here," I said, but Michael was already deep-breathing. I didn't need Zulaski to give me the story Michael's X-ray would tell. It would begin *once* and end *after.*

I got out of bed and passed Mrs. Flannery watching TV alone in the living room. She looked up, surprised.

"We're not brothers," I said.

She shrugged. "I had a son once."

The dead things on the wall stared at us. I wondered how she could stand their company, if it was possible that she was comforted by it. She liked talking animals.

"I'm going for a walk."

She handed me her husband's flashlight.

I could smell my tree as soon as I stepped outside. It had gotten even bigger, dropped more seeds that had sprouted into their own trees. My house was buried somewhere inside. It seemed like I'd been gone a longer time than I had. The tree was so tall I couldn't see the top of it. I imagined an ax, dense with sap, chopping ring after ring, never reaching the core.

I walked toward the house, flashlight beam bobbing along the ground. Birds flew overhead, some of them changing shape mid-flight. A girl in red darted by. I breathed with my tree and felt the wild things spreading seed. Mrs. Flannery was right: the foundation was shot. And the house wasn't empty. I could sense that much, but not who I'd find in my bed. Whether wolf or child; *don't talk to strangers* or *don't trespass.* Houses tell stories. Trees don't. I didn't investigate my house's new inhabitants, walked instead toward the massive trunk in the center of the wood. I'd known from an early age that stories for children didn't include boys like me. That I had to find my own way.

The flashlight shone on words carved into the bark. *Climb me.*

I wasn't going to return with golden eggs. I climbed anyway. There would be something for me at the top, or there wouldn't. I kept climbing.

In the morning I heard chainsaws buzzing far, far below.

THE FLOODED ROOM

The affair lasted longer than the marriage. I woke up one morning and realized that my lover had outlasted all of my other relationships. Marriage, divorce, courtship, second marriage: it was my mistress I loved. I called her that day.

"Trina," I said.

Crackle and static.

"Trina, I love you. It's always been you."

"I'm working on a problem," she said, and hung up. Math, she meant. She walked around with numbers following her. Her day job was thinking. My day job was her.

She called back that afternoon. My phone lit up: *Farrier.* When you're on the down low you need horseshoes for luck.

"I'm getting a divorce," I told her. "You're the love of my life."

"Numbers don't lie. Have you opened your mail?"

The envelope was thick as a book. Inside was a list of every minute we'd spent together over the past 9 years. At the bottom was a blank fifteen-minute slot.

"See that blank slot?"

Cue a sinking feeling.

"That's where I leave you. Our fifteen minute goodbye."

She left, and left the water running in the clandestine apartment we'd shared. I showed up the next day and found the carpet soaked. A mold guy showed up a few days later and tore up the carpet, sprayed the place with chemicals. Now it smelled antiseptic, hospital-dismal. I replaced the carpet with dark blue tile, a reminder that I was treading on a flood zone.

Every evening after work and before dinner with my wife I walked over to my secret apartment and sat at the built-in booth. It was that kind of apartment, kitschy. I imagined a gangster and the gangster's lover, a beautiful woman with a pearl-handled gun.

While I was pretending Trina was in the next room, taking a bath or touching herself, I glimpsed something beneath the stove. A strand of dark hair or the tip of a pencil. I got down on my knees and reached under the stove.

It was the number 9. She'd forgotten one of her numbers and now what? Her equation would go awry; the floating numbers would never line up.

I put the number 9 on the table, between the salt-and-pepper shakers. Trina was so organized; surely she'd know if a number went missing?

Nothing moved but the clock. I caught the blue line home.

Dinner was on the kitchen table, plate covered with another plate. Between our salt-and-pepper shakers was the number 3, a burning candle minus a cake.

"What's up with the number?"

"I thought that was yours."

That night my wife and I watched TV. I curled into her body like we were animals in a cave or soup cans on an end cap. It was all so easy, but I missed Trina's borderline personality. Why was it, I wondered, that one person could taste so good while another person, equally attractive and attentive, tasted like toast?

The first time Trina and I fucked, I buried my face between her legs and lost myself in the next nine years. Our secret apartment was flooded with sensory detail: verbena shampoo, orange-mint gum, strands of black hair on the blue-and-white quilt.

That night I dreamed Trina broke into my house and covered the walls with numbers.

The next day I walked my dog down Benson Street.

Benson Street was where Trina lived with whoever she lived with. She rented out rooms in her big gray house. My dog and I walked by, looked at the numbers nailed to the outside of the house. I had the 9 and the 3 in a grocery bag, fantasies of knocking on her door. *I just thought you might want these*, then, *oh, what is this?* and *I was wrong, so wrong, let's start over.*

No one answered the door. But I had a key.

In nine years, you learn a few things about a person. Like where to look for answers. What to take when you have the chance. I went straight to her study. Her organization made it easy. I took the file marked with my name, surprised that it wasn't bigger. I left everything else behind because, in nine years, you also learn what not to look at.

I slipped the file into the grocery bag, feeling the doors creak behind me, the windows watching. She'd spent more time in this room than with me. I left no record of my presence except the missing file. I expected that it would give me some answers, and that she would call when she discovered what I'd done.

I returned to the secret apartment, spread the spreadsheets on the floor, the 9 and the 3 floating in blue tile. The numbers in their boxes looked like pinned insects. The formulas were complicated, integers and differentials, theorems I couldn't remember. I poured coffee, kept reading. Penciled notes on a clipboard. Tried to work backward from her solutions.

She'd tracked everything, each day I'd left her early to get home on time, every minute I'd wasted, the ten long minutes I'd talked to her with lettuce in my teeth. Times when I'd been selfish in bed, times when I'd been too demanding, when I'd talked about my exes too much or not enough, when I hadn't paid my fair share, when I'd taken the last word, when I hadn't offered her a ride or a bite or a drink or a hand. The numbers added up perfectly. The only errors I saw were mine.

There had been so many right times to tell Trina I loved her.

Maybe it was all that staring, but after a while the numbers seemed to levitate off the page. A cross between 3D and a mirage. They peeled off the paper, wet and wrinkled. Gained substance, bloated, pulsed. They hung around me like a container. Some smooth, some slimy, some grainy and sweet-smelling. They snapped together, magnetized. Consumed each other. It was a whole ecosystem of numbers, and it crowded the room.

I had trouble breathing. I suspected the numbers were displacing the air.

I touched a 2; it went limp and slopped over my hand. Same thing with a 7. I'd expected a clatter and rubble. Maybe that I would be crushed. But time is not heavy like that. Soon I had a pile of shimmering numbers heaving on the floor like dying fish. The tiles began to sweat. My cell phone buzzed across the room, and I knew without looking that it was Trina. The condensation grew. I had to wade through piles of dying numbers to get to the phone. Everything turning to mush. The things I'd done right, the things I'd done wrong: disintegrating, disappearing.

I got to the phone just in time.

"Hello, Trina, I love you," I said.

Silence. Then, "My equation was off."

"Yes," I said, desperate. "Yes it was."

"Did you fix it?"

I didn't respond. I knew from my marriages and divorce that there was no right answer.

"The apartment," I said. "It's wrecked again."

"That makes sense," she said.

"It does?"

"Time's up." The line clicked off.

I called the cleaning company again, and said, "I don't know how to explain this, but I need help cleaning up a relationship."

"Messy break-up?" the voice on the line said.

"You've dealt with this before?"

"What's the nature of the damage? Love letter fire, tear-drop clog?"

"Numbers," I said. "They're all over."

"Unusual," the voice said. "Potential biohazard. We'll have someone over right away."

I thought they might be right. There was a black liquid oozing from the number piles now. They smelled faintly of mold. So I went home. My wife was holding a plate of toast when I walked in, and when she saw me she held her nose. "You stink. What happened to you?"

"I love you," I said.

"Well," she said and pursed her lips.

She took a big bite of toast, and I went to the shower to wash off the lie.

CORRESPONDING WITH FIRE

Jane starts a letter to her mother again. "Dear Mom"—immediately strikes the "Dear." They've never been that to each other and she doesn't want her tone to be interpreted as sarcastic; there's been too much of that already.

"Mom,"—too familiar. "Mother" seems more distant, more what she's going for, she thinks. "Mother" is closer to the sentiment, the kindest she can have, for a woman who hasn't spoken to her willingly in over seven years.

Both of her aunts say her mother is jealous.

"*Independence*—you do what you want and don't rely on anyone."

"She had two kids, ten and eight, by your age, you know."

Sometimes one of them, the aunts, will try to say her mother is proud of her, or would be if she knew enough to be. No one is convinced, least of all Jane, who sits at her desk and stares at her hands. Somewhere in there, she thinks, there must be some words beyond Dear and Mother or Mom. She is starting to question capitalization, starting to question Dear. What are the rules here?

Mothermothermother. "Mother,"—that sounds fine, if it can't be something stronger, some profanity rearticulated in type or "Denise," (another familiarity she can't get comfortable with. She never understood how the world didn't fall apart for kids who called their parents by name). She might use "Mrs. Zulaski," but she doesn't even know if that's true anymore. The divorce has been looming for two decades—almost since that snapshot of her, eight months pregnant on their honeymoon. There were never any tricks of mathematical calculations to be done trying to convince Louie he wasn't conceived out of wedlock. This, at least, is one number she can't fudge or ignore all together.

In the picture her mother is on the boardwalk in Atlantic City. She's backlit by the February sun's intensity dappling on the waves and beach behind her. From the photo one can't tell if she's glowing from this pregnancy the way women do. Her face is too much in shadow. The orange tip on the end of a short nub of cigarette peeks out from her hand, which has not completely worked its way into hiding behind her back. This is what Jane remembers most. There is a smile on her face that is filled with reserve.

She smoked when she was pregnant the first three times: with Ryan (but then, she was *just 19*), with Jane (apparently there may have been other substances—but early on—when she *wasn't sure*), Louis (as evidenced in the honeymoon photo), but not with Lynette, the last.

Jane's stepfather, Dr. Zulaski, was sure the last would be a girl. He started up a campaign to fight the smoking immediately, the day Denise peed on the stick. "That's fine for boys, they can handle it, but I want my girl turning out all right."

"Jane turned out fine."

"Depends on what you mean."

There was no mathematical pretense for this conversation either. Jane was ten years old, four feet from their side of the dinner table, and seven green beans from getting up.

In the news, another story about miners stuck inside the earth. By the time she hears about it, they are six days trapped. Briefly Jane wonders if it is her fault or weak media coverage on another corporate disaster that keeps the information from her. Jane puts a plastic bag over her head and breathes in and out slowly, slowly cinching the plastic around her neck. She tries to imagine what it would really be like if the air got thinner and thinner and there was no bag to come out of, no high-ceilinged kitchen and open window in which to find relief.

The pad of paper sits on the kitchen table, it's empty blue lines mocking. On the paper three words: Mother on one line, and I went on the line below.

Where did she go that would be worth mentioning?

During the yellow fever outbreak in the South in the late 1800s it was thought that mail carried the disease. As a result each letter was shipped by rail to an unpopulated rural area where postal workers would stop the train to fumigate the mail. The postmen would sweat deeply in the confines of dark lantern-lit boxcars, in which even the heat of an *early* Southern summer morning would be unbearable for more than a half-hour or so at a time. Here they would sit over the soft burlap of man-sized mail sacks, poking holes into each letter with a perforation paddle, thick scarves wrapped around their faces to protect their noses and mouths from breathing the correspondence in. Only after violating each envelope in this way did the men pump the sulfur in. Even children, recognizing the smelly work being done, would skirt a wide berth around these briefly dormant trains, only watching from a distance as yellow-orange wisps slipped from drafty cars and disappeared into the humid air.

When she was twelve she asked for gerbils. They were more like rats than the hamster Ryan had had. Jane liked their slender, nearly-hairless tails. And she was *much* more responsible than her brother. She promised the metal door would never be left open, that the gerbils would never leave the iron mesh of the three-story "Critter Condo" to be found months later (months after the search party—Ryan and Jane and Louie on their hands and knees everywhere—had been called off) decaying in the small pit in the back corner of the basement where the sump pump kicked on loudly after a heavy rain. By that time "Hamlet" wasn't much more than a few dry tufts of hair stretched over bone.

And they never did get out—Jane's gerbils Emerald and Midnight—they even died of old age. She was a successful parent. But her mother took a long time forgiving the sins of the sixteen-year-old boy working the pet store in the strip mall who sold her a male and a female instead of the two females like she'd asked for.

Every few months, more frequently in spring and summer, Jane would walk two miles back to the strip mall pet store with a shoebox full of black and brown gerbil offspring. They were not much bigger than a child's thumb, but had hair and long skinny tails.

They couldn't be given up right away. When they were born they were hairless, almost less-than dime-sized and see-through. Their flesh was dark pink in some places, but translucent where it stretched over their middle. In their chests one could see their red little hearts ticking quickly, and all the other organs. So like a human, Jane thought, but unbelievably small. If she touched them right away she was sure they would fall apart, their skin sticking to the whorls on the tips of her fingers, flesh ripping away from bone that was not yet entirely developed. Their hold on the world was vague and unconvincing and they made sounds like the chiming of tiny clocks.

Jane always tried to be home for the birthing. She learned the signals of labor with the diligence of a midwife, the low moans of the mother, the inability for her to sit still or to sleep. She would be like this usually the day before. And when the signs were evident the father, Midnight, had to be taken, by the base of the tail (because he was agitated too), so that he would not eat his children as the mother, Emerald, birthed them.

It was likely the babies were sold as snake food, like the baby mice were. An instant death only moments into the world probably would have been the most humane way for them to go, but the idea was too much for Jane at the time. Parents eating their children.

Jane wondered what prompted such a disturbing design in such a creature's mind and decided it was probably the smell. Even in all the insignificance of the babies' size the organic tinge of the event would linger in the room for two days until their mother cleaned them off enough. During this interim Jane would sleep in the hallway just outside her bedroom door, until she got used to the odor, or until it went away.

Most fascinated with the way, after the birthing process, Emerald would *eat* the afterbirth, Jane stood staring for as long as it took until the tiny tired animal pulled the mess of it up to her face in one string after another with the frenetic motion of her paws flitting around her tiny mouth. Jane would stand at the cage with her own girl parts pressed against an open dresser drawer.

One day, after the third or fourth litter of the season had been born, as she was feasting on the placenta, one of the newborns twisted and kicked his or her little transparent body around in just the wrong way to get mixed up in the middle of her eating. Jane watched in horror as Emerald swallowed her child, not even pausing to consider the variation in texture and taste from the rest of the meal. From then on Emerald and Midnight lived in separate quarters.

It is August, 1897. Somewhere near the border of Georgia and Alabama, between Columbus and Phenix City, a train catches fire.

Columbus has not yet, at this point, grown into much more than a large small town, but most residents maintain—as they will more than a hundred years later—that they are, in fact, a city. They are, they say, as metropolitan as Atlanta and Birmingham, only with less crime and less of a "negro" population (some say these two are related).

It is no unknown matter that these trains are passing through, from Atlanta to Birmingham—although this is not the most direct route. The cars shove through on their way to Tallapoosa County, Alabama, where the families that work the land are "likely inbred anyway," to kill the sickness that hides between sheaves of paper, parchment and plain lined, resting invisibly in lines of type and within swirls of delicate handwriting. No one here is happy these trains have been rerouted.

The train cars are sealed, they're told.

Without great concentration anyway it should bring no harm, the government explains of obvious fissures in some of the cars' metal walls, *besides, in open air it dissipates.*

Unmindful of the discordant sentiment of residents the trains rattle through. They slow within the city limits, following an ordinance since several inebriated townsfolk were drawn to the tracks tragically the year before. The slow clang and clatter of the axels riding the slight variations in the track are so regular in measure that they would be soothing if the train were carrying something else.

When people see the U.S. Postal Service logo, its three colors of American patriotism rarely in dull paint on the side of the boxcars, most residents shoulder themselves inside from whatever they were doing *just in case.* The streets are nearly deserted for the ten minutes it takes a train to pass completely through.

The firemen are quick to respond. They wear full facemasks for the first time ever with their heavy rust-colored jumpsuits *just in case.* When the train cars cool three men will be found inside one charred car, two inside another. All five men will be spread over blackened piles of letters—trying to keep the fever in.

By the end of June, Jane has finished the letter. Even after reading it three times she isn't sure what it says. She waits for the words to make sense. She turns the paper sideways so that the words form towers of graphite separated by blue lines. She turns it upside down and looks for anything to resemble words that way. In that way she makes out something that looks like "pus" and something else that looks like "strash," which isn't even a word, but makes more sense to her than the other things. The week of the fourth of July, Jane walks to the mailbox on the corner of her street, with the flap still open on the envelope and, understanding the words will never work out however she manoevers them, she seals the envelope and slips it into the blue trap door. The trap door squeaks shut like something living. Jane checks the door again to make sure the envelope with its pillars of words have really slipped inside. That night someone throws a handful of firecrackers into the mailbox on the corner of Jane's street. The pyrotechnics exploding inside the blue box sound like heavy artillery fire for the minute or so it takes for them to wear themselves out. All the mail is burned, black smears of carbon slide from every seam.

DAMAGE CONTROL

I kissed my girls and Dan goodbye and drove to my girlfriend's house to fight. I did it for the money. I did it because I was good at it. I did it because I wanted to know how to take care of myself, in case the *what if* always playing in my head came to pass. I did it because there was something in me that cried out to strike, and I was against spanking.

I don't know why I did it.

I couldn't stand to be in my house, so I got in the car and drove, and when I drove, I didn't have anywhere else to go but Cat's house across town. Nothing was open that late. Just all-night groceries and bars, and there are only so many groceries a person can buy.

Cat's door was always unlocked because she lost the key and didn't want to pay the landlord to get a new one, so I let myself in. She was asleep in the tub, cell phone still attached to some call. I put the phone to my ear. "Hello?"

"You're back."

"Who is this?"

"It's me."

A man's voice; a client. I felt sorry for the guy, waiting on her to return like Dan had waited on me. He thought I was going through something. He thought I would eventually stop going through it and return to him. He didn't realize this was a new way of life for me, had been since shortly after my second was born. That I couldn't come home to him in the morning if I didn't fight.

I wished the guy on the line good luck and hung up.

"Wake up," I said to Cat, but she didn't budge. I tried to imagine her as a child, or a fetus sleeping in water. It was hard to imagine because of her tattoos, blackbirds and hyenas and fish with teeth. It was important for me to picture her as a child so I didn't forget empathy. I could tell I was forgetting because of how hard it was to see her as someone's daughter, especially because she had no family. No parents, no siblings. Hard to picture someone loving her as a kid when maybe no one had.

But important for me to try.

I splashed water in her face. "Cathy. Get up."

She sputtered, breasts bobbing in the water. Her phone buzzed. The air conditioner kicked on, and she shivered. "Cold tub. Cold tub." At home, nets full of plastic toys hung from the showerhead and toothbrush holders were suction-cupped to the mirror. Cat's counter was crammed with open-capped muscle creams and gauze packages and painkillers and spilled butterfly bandages. Everything covered in a thick coat of old hairspray. Beer bottles in the sink.

"You ever clean in here?" I reached for a towel balled against the wall, sniffed it, grimaced.

She rolled herself over the side of the tub and groaned. Paused on hands and knees, water streaming off her and running into the floor vents. "A hello would be nice."

"I told the dude on the phone hello."

"That's a work phone."

"Was he paying to hear you sleep?"

She took the towel from me and wrapped herself in it, sat back on her heels. "He said it relaxes him. You should try it; it's the cure for what ails you."

"That's not how I relax."

She went into the bedroom and put on yoga pants and a sports shirt. We looked like two mid-thirties women about to go jogging around a lake or something. All that effort with no payoff. The thing about fighting was the release. Afterward

Cat and I always fucked. And once my aggression and libido had been expressed, I could go back to being a good wife and mother of two darling girls, Sid and Fig, ages two and four. Sid was obsessed with mermaids, Fig a budding veterinarian. The lights of my life, as long as my life included nights at Cat's house.

We called it Fight Club for Moms.

We called it Survival Training.

We called it Game Night.

We called it Therapy.

We called it Damage Control because, although we didn't have statistics, we were sure these meetings lowered the divorce rate and made us kinder to our children. When you see some woman at the co-op with a baby strapped to her chest, gently reminding her toddler that *screaming is not a choice,* and you think she is the picture of calm and peaceful motherhood, check her arms for bruises. She's probably one of us.

From the bedroom, I heard the front door open, and a voice call, "Anybody home?"

"Megan's here," I said. "Show time."

Megan sauntered into the bathroom, knee and elbow pads strapped into position, halter top duct-taped in place.

"You fighting tonight, Cat?"

"When's the last time I said no?"

"How about you, Lanie?"

"Ready for more."

"That's what Cat tells me." Megan slapped my ass.

"How's Bruiser?"

"Still trying to convince Johnny she walked into a door."

We called it Girl Time.

We called it Time Out.

Cat's clients called her slow voice sleep. I thought of Cat's fist balled up to strike, then coiled tighter until it opened inside me. We didn't call it love, just violence. Nothing I needed to fess up to Dan. He'd say sex with a girl didn't count. He'd say *What's for dinner* and *Where's the remote?*

Cat opened a beer and tossed me her car keys. I covered my sports bra with a fake fur coat. My mom would say *Don't leave the house like that, Lanie.*

Now I was the mom and I left all the time.

We fought in an abandoned concrete factory on the edge of town, train tracks competing for a view of the bay. In fading light I recognized Bruiser's van. Megan took off around the back of the factory. We could've pried open the front door, but everyone used a broken window instead.

Cat jumped off the dusty sill, then reached a hand to pull me over. Together we raced toward voices and light. Our fights took place in the storeroom, illegally rigged for electricity courtesy of Bayview Electric. Beyond us, women pressed against a stage cordoned off with rope. We couldn't see who was in the ring, but the noise told us the fighting was ugly.

Megan and Bruiser stood kissing by the beer cooler, legs intertwined. Bruiser's real name was Tiffany Williams. She worked part-time as a dental hygienist.

"Does it bother Bruiser to see teeth knocked out?"

"Does it bother you?"

"Someone could die."

Cat shrugged. "If someone goes down, she deserves to go down. We brought her here because of what she did."

Cat was right. Sorry didn't mean the same thing when you were punched in the face as it did when you were reading a letter. And they always got a letter first. A letter, a phone call, and a meeting in person.

The buzzer sounded. Our girl Janine swaggered out of the ring, arms raised, bleeding from the mouth. The room erupted while the other girl stumbled, fell to her knees, and clung to the rope.

Sometimes someone took care of the ones who fell, but sometimes we just let them bleed. The referee dragged the girl out of the ring and dropped her on a chair by the cooler.

Janine cracked a beer and wiped her bloody mouth on

her bicep.

Later the girl would crawl to her car. Drive halfway home, catch a cab to the hospital. She'd describe the accident exactly as scripted. The script was simple. The script was key.

"What if someone tells the truth?"

Cat had been fighting much longer than me. "She fights again, but not in the ring. When she least expects it. And no referee."

Sometimes they had to be coaxed or dragged. Sometimes they cried and curled up in a corner. The best fighters were raging mad, too angry and arrogant to believe they might lose.

The loudspeaker crackled. "Next match coming up. Home court advantage: Megan!"

We cheered until our throats went raw.

"Tonight's opponent comes to us from Ferndale. Please welcome Cindi!"

The lights flickered and the back door opened. Time for someone to walk in blind. Misled thinking it was a bridal shower for a friend of a friend of a very bad friend.

A tall blonde woman strode into the room like she was expecting a party. Her heels ricocheted against the concrete floor. She stopped dead in front of the ring. "Billy? Billy, is this a joke?"

She scanned the room, pacing. It was the only sound and it echoed strangely. We watched while Cindi lost her cool, while the referee dragged her into the ring.

The panicky moments were always Cat's favorite. "Like hunting," she said, "but I don't even eat meat."

"Where am I?" Cindi veered off balance, dizzy. Dropped her pocketbook. A lipstick rolled between the ropes. Megan stared and flexed and waited for Cindi's heels to come off. No shoes, no jewelry. No scarves up our sleeves.

The referee pushed Cindi toward the center of the ring. Megan jogged in place, punching at nothing.

"You?" Cindi shook her head. "You're Andrew's mom. You wrote that letter."

"Your kid's a bully."

"Your kid's a sissy."

"My kid tried to hang himself from a tree out back. Thank god the branch broke. But your kid pushed him to it."

Cindi brushed her hair over her shoulder. "Maybe if your kid had a father he'd know how to take a joke."

Megan ran at her. Cindi flailed, slapping and snarling like she'd bite.

She bit.

Megan locked her wrists around Cindi's neck, pulled her head into her chest, and kneed her in the chin so hard we heard the snap.

"One!" yelled the ref.

We counted out loud.

Cindi pounded the mat.

We called it a tap out.

Bruiser picked up Megan and twirled her around.

Back home Sid and Fig were sleeping, dreaming of fish with teeth and animals chasing each other around a room lit by burning ropes.

"Your turn," Cat whispered, wrapping me in her blackbird arms.

AMNESIAC LUNG

Mostly women afflicted, mostly caretakers. Something in the air doesn't sit right in our chests. We're supposed to take calming breaths. Our Loved Ones are supposed to remind us. It behooves Our Loved Ones to remind us, but they often forget. That's when we wake up in hotels in Poughkeepsie, in Bithlo, in Ocean City, we wake up in the back seat of a rented Pathfinder, we wake up in boxer briefs or prom dresses, we wake up in the middle of binges and one night stands, and we don't remember how we got there. We call home—*fine, not a scratch, splitting headache*—and charge the fare to the credit card number tattooed on our arms. Begin the exhausting recovery.

Our Loved Ones foot the bill.

We can tell they sort of think we're faking.

It can happen anytime, and later we won't remember the onset. Our Loved Ones tell us how we dropped them off at school, at the office, at the chiropractor, at the therapist, how we kissed them goodbye and waved, and if they noticed a slightly different breathing pattern, they don't say. Routines vary among us, but every woman has her habits: clothes in a duffel, meds doled out, dog to the boarder, bank account cleared.

Mine was a Big Gulp and a full tank.

Mine was kids to their dad's and a crossbow in the trunk.

Mine was emails days later from Clark and Dan and Steve, *You coming to get this buck?* and my response, *I'm sor-*

ry, I don't know who you are, I'm a vegetarian.

My hypnotherapist says something inside me is calling for sacrifice. My psychic says I was a war veteran in a past life. My doctor says I'm anemic. My girlfriend says I prepare tofu so well she barely misses meat. She cleans out the fridge and goes on all-night benders while I drive across town to my ex's to nurse the baby. Shared custody means Aaron the Ex doesn't have to bring the baby to me on his days, and Amanda the Girlfriend doesn't ever have to see the kids if she doesn't want to. It's a win-win for everyone but me.

Aaron and I divorced because, while he said he could deal with my girlfriends, he couldn't get over the late-night texts from strange men complimenting me on my skills and wanting to know where I'd learned to shoot like that. Aaron wondered that, too, but I didn't know the answer. In real life, I'm squeamish. I don't like cleaning up my own kids' bloody knees, and I was never the one to give the diabetic cat her daily shot. Even after three kids and at least as many girlfriends, it was the unknown that Aaron couldn't handle. He'd been a stay-at-home dad; now he was a stay-at-his-home dad. He sued for full custody, said I was an unfit mother, but the judge said he couldn't prevent me from visiting the kids because of my condition. He *could* insist on supervised visits, so of course he did.

For a while, even the sound of Aaron's voice set off my AL, his words like a clamp on my airways. Blackouts lasted days instead of hours. Tonight I stop on my way to Aaron's to pick up my chaperone. She's middle-aged but dresses like a much older woman: rain cap and skirt with an elastic waist. Her AL has been in remission so long that she's considered recovered. She'd been a mild case to begin with, long walks on the beach when she was supposed to be watching the kids, and after her divorce her symptoms went away. Tonight she wants to know if I've had any episodes, so as I drive I tell her about waking in the lodge, animal heads on the walls. Camo head to foot. Sometimes I'll wake in my own room, and then I can sneak away without trouble. This time, I'd come to in mid-conversation: a gasp, and the stares of half a dozen dudes, the kind of guys I'd never hang with normally. I felt like I hadn't breathed in days. The telltale headache. I drained a glass of someone else's water and excused myself. Dogs baying on my walk to the car, which I always parked in the same spot.

We're almost to Aaron's house by the time I'm finished telling her. I park in the driveway.

"You okay?" Clarisse says.

I look at the house, my children secreted somewhere inside. "Will be soon," I say.

The door opens on my grinning boy. "Mommy," he says. His father is behind him, holding the baby. My oldest girl looks up from the TV. The house is bathed in soft light, smells like bubble bath. Just the sight of the baby causes the milk to let down, so I grab my chest to hold it in, feel my lungs contract. I want my easy, old life back, before Girlfriend Number Two did that thing with her tongue and ruined me for Aaron, Aaron of the bubble baths, backrubs, footie pajamas. Sweet Aaron, who wouldn't watch porn if I paid him.

My ribs move closer together: cage.

"I'm just going for a little drive," I tell Clarisse, and I'm out the door, rattling my keys.

When I wake up, it's morning. The pillow beside me gurgles and purrs. I stumble out of bed, whack my knee on a dresser. Feel for a light switch, which clicks on too brightly, waking me and my companion both.

At first I think she's sick, because she's strapped to some kind of breathing machine. Then she sits up, pulls the tube out of her nose.

"Sleep apnea. This thing with my throat."

Skyscrapers press against our window. Plush patterned carpet cushions my feet. There's a velvet loveseat and a wet bar, and it looks like we used both between falling and waking.

My lungs feel swollen; it hurts to breathe. The telltale headache. Big Gulp in the sink.

"You were incredible last night." Her mouth twists up at the corner, tiny scar over her lip, and I remember that scar in my mouth, laughing while she kicked off her shoes.

I rummage a pamphlet from my purse. "I have this disease? It's not contagious? It's called AL? Maybe you saw the film?"

"C'mere." She crooks her finger my way.

"It was called *My Lungs Led Me To You.* It had a happy ending. That actress with the gigantic mouth, she was really good."

"C'mere, Cindy."

My name isn't Cindy, but it could be. And I'm wide awake, and I remember some things.

She ties her hair in a knot on top of her head, pulls on hot pink velour sweats, grabs her purse from the dresser. We take the elevator down to the lobby. Coffee's expensive, big city prices. I use the credit tattooed on my arm. While she's in the bathroom I scan for a newspaper, but everyone's wired, reading online.

The guy beside me smiles, so I blurt out: "Excuse me; I just woke up from a coma. What year is it and what's our address?"

He laughs, and the guy sitting beside him laughs, and the two women behind them laugh, and everyone thinks my real life is funny. My headache booms. I swear there's a taxidermy deer hanging over the condiment table.

I think of my crossbow, blood in my trunk.

Maybe my kids are in college, maybe it's time to let go.

Sleep Apnea comes back from the bathroom, bright red lipstick and rhinestone barrettes. She looks into my eyes like she's searching for something.

"What year is it and what's our address?"

When she tells me, I write it down on my arm. I've been gone so long, and I'm so far from my children.

She reaches for my hand across the table. That's when I notice her ring, a thick gold band.

"I knew the minute I saw you."

Her ring matches the ring on my left ring finger.

"I still can't believe it. I'm calling my Mom." She punches numbers into her cell. "Mom? It's Ruth. Guess what? I'm hitched!" There's talk of cake, guests clinking glasses. We both wore dresses: mine tailored, hers lace. Our registry was practical, with a few whimsical touches thrown in. When we danced to our song, the DJ cried.

We take the elevator back up to the 14th floor. As I unlock the door Ruth pauses.

"Must've left my purse downstairs. I'll be right back, Honey." Throws me a kiss as the elevator sways.

I hope the kids like her. I'm gathering my wife's clothes from the floor and stuffing them in her suitcase. This isn't how I thought my second marriage would begin, but isn't love always a gamble, a test?

I'm hanging out on the 14th floor, hundreds of stairs uphill, imaginary flames shooting from the balcony.

I call Aaron collect.

"Where are you?" he asks. "I've been worried sick."

"If I were on the 14th floor of a hotel, and the hotel was on fire, would you come get me?"

"Sweetheart, cut the crap."

"Are you dating Clarisse?"

His silence says yes.

"I'm not coming home this time."

My lungs say that something inside me is calling for forgiveness. My heart says that I was a terrible parent in a past life. My ring says I'm a blushing bride.

I dial the front desk. "Fire," I say.

Sirens, doors slamming, an insistent alarm. The elevator's off limits, but the stairs are illuminated with a bright red *EXIT.*

This time I'm not just forgetting, I'm forgotten. Some people weren't meant for children, for bubble baths, for the life I remember in exquisite detail. I know exactly where I am: in a hotel burning a hole in this city, ready to breathe in the scent of the new.

I get into bed and crawl under the covers. Wait to see if she'll climb.

VARDA

"Elizabeth Taylor wasn't an alien."

"How do you know?"

"*Butterfield 8.*"

"Fine. You don't have to believe me. I'm just sharing more, like our therapist said."

"Sharing doesn't mean pretending."

"I'm not pretending."

"You're not an alien."

"You're embarrassing me."

"Do aliens blush?"

"I don't blush, but some of us do."

"So now it's us, like you know other aliens."

"We notice each other."

"By sight?"

"By smell."

After dinner I stared in the mirror while I flossed, wondering what it would feel like to have sex with an alien. Of course, we both knew you weren't really an alien. But even sharing pretend things made me feel closer to you. Like something was shifting in the direction of love. Like things might change and go back to what was.

That night we kissed more than usual. You smelled like violet talcum powder.

"What do aliens smell like?"

"It's not really a smell. We have more senses than humans do, so we have to use the closest approximate sense to describe them. It's actually varda."

"Varda?"

"Like human smell, but it's also a kind of touch, except that we don't actually physically touch each other."

"Wow. Like tantra?"

"More like TV."

You were always so imaginative. Not like me, with my boring desk job and my boring lunches and my boring ways.

"Do aliens have pets?"

"We carry them with us."

"Like teacup poodles?"

"Like ferrets. They stink."

"Do they talk?"

"They whisper, but we can't understand them. Mostly they vibrate and keep our hearts warm."

"But now you have Fido."

You smiled and called Fido. Rubbed his ears and scratched his chin.

"We're not that bad," I said. "We domesticated dogs. Gotta admit, Earth's pretty great."

You went into the bathroom and ran the shower, but didn't take a shower. Then you got into bed without saying goodnight.

The next morning you left for work early and texted to say you'd be home late.

But Dr Zulaski

Cant make appt

2 late 2 cancel

You go instd

So I went by myself. The waiting room was full of couples. People were reading and checking their phones.

Dr. Zulaski looked at me quizzically when he opened the door on just me.

"Emily got stuck at work."

"I see," he said.

I sat in my chair, the high-backed wooden chair I always sat in, but then decided to try your chair, instead. It was so comfortable. I never knew.

"What issues came up for you this week?"

I wasn't sure where to start, so I told Dr. Zu about your hilarious alien identity prank. He listened quietly and didn't laugh once. After a while I felt stupid for telling a joke he wasn't getting.

"Emily isn't really an alien."

Dr. Zu listened.

"I mean, we're both just human. Like you."

Dr. Zu made notes on a yellow pad.

"Emily gets very clown college sometimes."

"Clown college?" Dr. Zu looked up, alert.

"It's an expression. It means someone's funny."

"Like clowns or like college?"

"Like clown college."

"I see."

More note taking, then I talked about my mother. At the end of the session Dr. Zu held the door open for me, then paused.

"I'd like to do an individual session with Emily. After that you should come as a pair."

I felt rejected, but tried not to show it. Even in therapy I was just the plus one.

Over dinner I brought up the fact that your chair was more

comfortable than mine.

"That's one of our senses."

"Varda?"

"No, tang."

"You have a sense named tang? Like that astronaut drink?"

"Where do you think it got its name?"

I almost believed you, and saw the flicker of a conspiracy theory where every U.S. brand name was alien code. "You're really convincing with this alien thing."

You smiled. One side of your face drooped slightly. Symmetry had never seemed sexy, so when I met your face, I fell in love with both sides. Your eyes were chocolate-colored, with green flecked galaxies.

"Tell me another alien word."

"Kleenex," you said. "It means something like love."

"The brotherly kind? Or the kind that leaves bruises?"

There it was, blue fading into lemon.

I spun my own secret past orbiting worlds.

I AM LOLITA LUX

I am Lolita Lux. I changed my name to Laura. I sometimes go by Larry, but Joshua likes this not at all. I am Larry-not-Larry, Lolita-not-Lolita. And my mother calls me Lola.

She has not visited yet. When we talk on the phone it's really only her talking until she gets to something she doesn't know—usually a news item. I scan the papers so I can fill her in. "I know just what that Middle East stuff is all about, Mom," I say. "You just fix the planes." And while the word Mom rolls around feeling weird in my mouth I think about the thick bodies of planes with snub noses and jets that get pointy at the end. I think about the sound barrier and how I have no idea how fast you have to go to get there. Fast. She works at the base doing something; she has clearance. Josh says her hands are always scrubbed impeccably clean. That's what he talks about when he talks about her, crescent moon of fingernails. And she laughs. And her dog barks. And then she has to go. She has. No. Idea.

I married up when I snagged Josh. Joshua, Joshua. Not remembering the ua may be the thing that gets me caught. He is a hedge fund manager. I have no idea what he does. His hair is dark blonde and one hundred dollars dye each month to get it how it is. His physique is too perfect for someone who sits in a chair all day. His chair is leather—or something is—I can smell it on him when he walks in the door. Like clean horses. Or new shoes. And the light girlie scent of his cologne or hair products. I would call him metrosexual except for the hard swing of his hand. A wanna-be fag would never hit his girl. It's not abuse if it's in the bedroom and asked for. No, not that way. I mean really. Really saying it, "please baby, please," "harder," and "more." On my knees, ass in the air. The first time I saw him last month I wanted to show my ass to him. Wanted him to warm it with the hot heavy flat of his hand. We've been married seven years. He says he's never breathed like this. He says he's never—

This thing about the bus? A formality. The means to an end. Convey me from point A to point B. Like a bus. Yes, just like that.

The man on the bus with the little dog—now my dog, my dog, my Elodie, my Ely—was yelling into the phone. Little dog huddled deeper in shadow. I shifted my feet, crossed and uncrossed. Something about the fishnets itching. Crossed, I decided. Oh, the sweat that will gather between legs.

It had been a long night, like they all were. Grunts between notes, and men's whistles like the sound of rigging knocking a ship's side. Sometimes all I wanted was a boat in the harbor. Sometimes I wanted to be the boat, sometimes the harbor. I just wanted someone who could fuck good, hit hard, and pay for things. Didn't matter boy or girl. In Carlton I got both, which was good, but Carlton could be soft sometimes, could be too doting. All this I thought while I absently fingered the bite mark he'd left on my hip a few days before.

There is nothing like checking your wounds in public. And here I was on the bus again, poking at a bruise.

Home, I said. Home will be a headache, but it will be a fresh one and it will be mine. That's all we can say about a life sometimes, that it's ours. Until one day it isn't.

The cold day drifted by outside the greasy windows, cold and young. The sun battled it out with the clouds to come up. The man snarled, clearly upset—I could read that this was not his natural mode. I shifted my legs again and looked up. The girl was staring at me. Again. So many mornings, this.

Carlton called her doppelganger after seeing her once;

sometimes he asked about her. "Everybody's got one." It's just that we don't usually see ours four times a week. She was all me in the face, and lean body, strong. Her makeup was plain, face a little mute and pale. The hair a little off. I cut my own neat bangs, a little shorter than hers. You could tell she paid serious money to get hers done. And I wanted to unbutton the top two buttons of her shirt to make her stop drowning in clothes.

The man hung up, red-faced from anger or embarrassment. I was looking at him. I looked to my feet, shifted again. Then there was a shriek, then a thud, then both he and the girl were suddenly gone.

How did I get there? Inside someone's car, pushing through snow drifts at the side of the road. Inside someone's car, heater thrumming some clicking noise. "A leaf," the woman said. How did I get there? "Lolita?" the woman said. There was a whimper in the back. Inside someone's car, breath wetting the window, fog. Wet came down, puddle across the rubber strip at the window's base. "Lolita?" But who was that? I felt my forehead, damp. Blood? I pulled away, not sure if it hurt. Not sure if I felt anything. "Lolita?" Who? "Who?" I finally said. "Oh dear," the woman said. Inside some strange car, wet dog smell, something burning. No, some heat lifting from the top of my foot. My foot bent sideways, something bulging. What had happened? "Who?" I said again. The dog whimpered softly. I turned around. "Who?" I said. "That's your dog," the woman said. "My dog." I said. "Elodie, Ely." "The tag says 'Angel.'" "Well isn't she?" I said. "Isn't she?" "She—" the woman said. "I'm taking you to the hospital," the woman said. "So many people injured," she said. "And I was right behind." "Is there?" I said. "Am I bleeding?" "Just a little bit. That's why they let you leave the scene." The scene. What happened? "Is there someone I can call, Lolita?" I said nothing. "Is there someone I can call?" I thought about Carlton sleeping, sleeping inside his rented room, the windows blacking the dim day out. No. I thought about neighbors. No one near who knew me. No one to call. "Lolita?" "Who?" I said. The woman held a wallet in her hand, flipped open to a photo, flipped open to a tiny box of me-not-me on a drivers license. Her. Oh. I thought, oh. I could be her. I could—"Yes," I said. "Yes, what?" the woman said. "Yes, Lolita."

He picked me up. But before. White sheets, white coat, white lights, bright. Change of clothes in her bag. Change of. I bet for spilling things. She feared the being sticky. Being dirty. The imperfection of a brown splotch of soy latte on her shirt, on her pants. The possibility of. She didn't— The clothes were just the same as the ones she had had on. The pants were the same. Simple, beige. The shirt was the same. White, or light pink. I couldn't—Things were foggy. I couldn't tell. Colors. Stitches moving. In the hospital the lights strobed overhead. Like what insects see. Their shutter eyes at sixty times per second. I'd heard that once. Where would I— Oh, I don't know. I put them on. Times per second. I took the blooded ones off, held the bed to hold up my ankle. Fucking hurt. Doctor gave me something for the pain that slurred me. "Someone is coming to get you." It was maybe a question. I didn't know. "Someone is—" I said. Then sat back down. "Your dog is outside with your friend," the doctor said. A friend? Is outside? "The woman who brought you," he said. Neat little man in a white coat, white incisors. "She has your dog." "Elodie." "Elodie must be a very good friend." "No," I said, "Ely." The doctor went away then and I pushed my damaged clothes into the bin at the side of the bed. It wasn't marked hazardous and the blood was all over them and some woman came in a minute later and paused and then took them. Fishnets creeping over the edge of the bin like cobwebs or some other useless thing. They weren't itching me anymore. These clean pants. I was—

And like that, I was someone else. All it took was clean pants. And the slippers the hospital gave. Fresh. New. I walked out into the snow. They weren't ready for me to go, but there was so much going on. They said, watch me. They would have to. Just for a little while. No sleeping. Lightly concussed.

No sleeping. I would have to tell my husband, is what they said. No sleeping. If they didn't tell him. No sleeping. How could they keep track. I went out to the car and got my dog. I thanked 'my friend' I waited on the curb with her while she smoked cigarette after cigarette and threw conversation at me like tossing spare change in a fountain. Pennies first, the weather, what day it was, almost the weekend, weekend plans. Then bigger coins, she told me her name, she told me her husband was a track coach, she told me the house that he bought. She told me nothing about herself. Because she was missing too? How nice is what I kept saying. How nice. How nice. She blew her smoke up into the air and it was gone. And it was gone. I watched after it like it was maybe caught beneath the awning or some bit of ledge, but it was gone. And she snubbed the lit end out on the trash can each time, felt the tip to be sure, then threw it in there. Then touched another one to her lips, then touched it to flame and then blew smoke up. And then it disappeared.

I may have slept standing up. And the next thing I knew I was in his car. Our car, our car. I was in our car. And the dog was whimpering in the back seat. "That woman said this dog was yours," Joshua said. And I thought and me, who told you I was yours, and we just go on believing? And I fell asleep. And we did.

When I woke up we were in slow traffic, the clouds were thick, different than they had been before. When you live here—

Thoughts were slow in coming. When you live here you get to recognizing the differences in clouds. Like mothers understand the cries of their babies. What it means, where it's going, what is called for.

The post-it note on the floor of the car said many things. It said spinach, it said wheat bread, it said butter, it said eggs, it said gel. I wondered at each of these things. Canned or fresh spinach, or maybe frozen, which I used for recipes when I made anything calling for anything. I wanted to know why he specified wheat when reserving space on this list for the bread. Did white call to him? Sourdough? Would he be irresponsible with his bread choice if he didn't indicate which? Or was this list written by her for him? Or him for her? For me? Butter seemed clear in and of itself and for that I was glad. There it was, third in a list of five. Right in the middle like an anchor, holding the rest of the list, the rest of the world together. Eggs. I always get free-range because I like to think about happy chickens clucking in the dust. Gel could mean a couple of things. I looked at his hair. Slick yes, but gel seemed so early 90s. And he was hipper than that. Maybe he meant toothpaste. Or maybe I wasn't up on my hair care products and people really were using gel, they were using hairspray even, hidden in bathrooms I would never see.

I couldn't tell which way the sky was coming, all dumb and all numb, though I kept telling myself we were on the five so we were going north, we were going north, which we mostly were. Meteorologists call the weather hour to hour. Will the cloudbank push in over land, up the hills and away? Will they reveal a clear sky? Or are the mountains pushing down on us?

In my apartment on the hill, up top on 45th, I can exit my door, pushing the mat in to prop, to not lock myself out when the swing-shut door closes shut. The mat to jam it. Walk to the end of the hall to the window that sees downtown, sees the needle, the water, sees the peninsula sometimes, mountains fading, sometimes non-existent, sometimes clear. I can watch the weather move. But in the 'burbs who knows which way the wind blows or which way is west, which way out, which way down?

"Is it supposed to rain today?" I asked him, my husband.

"Snow."

"Is it supposed to snow?"

"More, yes, so they say."

So they say is not something I had ever said before. The meteorologists? Other people in the hospital he may have talked to? People at his place of work where he had just come from to come and get me?

He reached for my hand and ended up on my leg.

Whether he rubbed my leg to feel the fabric or to comfort me, he rubbed my leg. Not long. Just back and forth long enough to know he'd made contact, been there, before moving on. He ran his hand over the wheel as though thinking, as though getting the feel of my leg or the feel of the fabric off his hand.

Does he love me? I thought. Does he know I'm not who I am.

Traffic slowed more at Lynnwood. North, I thought.

I thought I might tell him.

Traffic came to a stop.

"Christ," he said.

I opened my mouth to maybe tell him my name. Not Lolita: the something else. What was it again?

"You should sleep," he said.

"Probably an accident," he said a moment later.

"Another one," he said, indicating either mine or what we had just seen at the side of the road. Busted fender, tow truck, red flare in the wet and dirty reeds.

We had that discussion again, Carlton and I, the afternoon before or two afternoons before. The way days bleed. And life becomes not the accumulation of days, just a rapid switching on and off of the light of the sun. One short day masquerading as something that changes, something to change.

"What are we?" Carlton had said.

"Oh Jesus."

"What?"

"Why can't we just—"

"What?"

"Be."

I felt my breasts pushing out from my shirt. Sore, present, pushing. The top two buttons undone. I wondered was he watching me?

I looked over. He was looking at the road, slowly going nowhere, home. I wondered what our house looked like.

How did he not know? Just by the buttons even, how? What scars would I have that didn't match up to hers when the clothes came off? Or were they, were we one of those closed off couples who did what they needed to do in the dark so that the body could be any body imagined? It was conceivable he had already slept with me in this way, if they had come into the club, if he had. If he had seen me as some other version of her. But would he expect this? Someone who maybe looks like her, banged up and looking like her and riding in his car?

His hand on the gearshift. It was automatic. But he hovered his hand there lightly like he was used to having more control. The dog snored lightly in the back. Or was it the road rumbling under sticky tires?

"Do you have snow tires?" I asked. Every question seemed the key to everything, unlocking him.

"You know we do."

I could tell it had been a conversation. About money? Or did I not drive?

"I—" I said.

He turned to look at me. Dark eyes like dark, like storm clouds, but blue. What was I going to say? I love you? Try that on for size. I had said and done more intimate things with people I didn't know.

I put my head back again, closed my eyes, said something like "so sleepy." Opened my eyes. Then, "the doctors told me not to sleep."

Him: "What?"

"For twelve hours at least."

"Then don't sleep. Why didn't you tell me?"

"I am telling you now."

"This is what I mean." Some past conversation.

I paused. Looked out the window. What was the right thing to say? What is what you mean?

"I know," I said. "I'm sorry."

He looked at me, surprised. Like it wasn't supposed to be that easy. Like he waited for something more from me, something unpleasant. What was that supposed to be? How to fill this moment? I looked at his hand. What was I to say here, come back with? What was wrong with him / the thing I was supposed to hit back with?

I put my hand on his. He flinched, pulled back like I was some hot thing, put his hand back down.

"I want things to be different," I said.

But maybe he will ask me how?

He folded his hand over, curled it in mine.

"You know I love you, right?" he said.

"I know."

We stayed that way all the way home.

L.

CHAPTER ONE

Mother named me Lolita. It came from somewhere other than the novel, a fairy tale or a song kids sing at school. I was an excuse to use it. My given name. And our surname, Lux.

After a time I took another name, because by seventh grade kids knew there was something wrong with Lolita. The name was off; everyone could hear it. Even without reading the book they knew. When high school began I gave out my middle name like candy. I had no friends, so there was no one to retrain.

We lived east of Deception Pass, on the second largest American island. Long and skinny like a bride's pale arm. We were in the center of it all, the crooked elbow. Tiny house with a tree in the middle. Mother built the house around a tree, a round house to surround us. Noise covered us like a scratchy blanket when the Navy planes landed at Ebey's Reserve.

Mother seemed most alive when the planes hit the strip. She fixed whatever went wrong with their wings.

I don't believe in American myths about childhood. If you have an imagination, you're not innocent. I knew then what I know now I just didn't have the words to explain. The island was prison and womb, my mother was angry, and the planes flew bombs and soldiers to war.

CHAPTER TWO

What you must know is that I killed myself on accident. I had a name, a man, a house. Every morning I packed my lunch and caught the 7:13 bus into the city. From there I walked, bought a coffee at my favorite café. Then to campus, I settled behind my desk at the library. My job was involved, but not overly so. Plenty of time to daydream and listen. Other lives unfolded around me while I answered phones and checked email. I wanted a different life, but couldn't imagine what to do with the one I had. It had never felt right. Not the name, not the man, or the house. Occasionally at lunch with a friend I'd complain vaguely about the man or the house. They both wanted too much. Too much attention. Everything seemed so solid. Secure.

My friends, mostly single, couldn't see why this was bad. "Joshua really loves you," they'd say, touching my shoulder. And it was true. What do you say to that? Their stories about bar life made love sound like war. I didn't know what I wanted, only what bored me, all talk about dinner, debates about babies, the endless TV, sports matches or chef shows, rom-com or drama, and the hearty rotations of upset and anger.

So I kept on, and might've kept on forever, until the ice and blind, slipped wheels, until the accident gave me a split second's chance.

The 7:13 bus started in Everett, where we lived, and traveled forty minutes to downtown Seattle. The riders were commuters, like me. Over time we came to nod and exchange glances. Among the familiar faces was a woman who kept squarely to herself, withdrawn. She stared out the window. No wedding ring, no dog hairs, no sign of home. Her hair was long and black, like mine, with the same Bettie Page bangs. Dyed, like mine, so we both etched our eyebrows in. Tall, like me, and curvy. She wore thrift store 1950's dresses, fishnets, and boots. Once one of my co-workers sat next to her and began talking to her, thinking she was me. We were nearly identical. But whenever I caught her eye, she looked away. I thought about time travel movies and how you aren't ever supposed to meet yourself. What they call paradox.

On the morning of the accident Joshua and I had a fight. I wanted a dog; he did not. He wanted a baby. A dog was a distraction, he said.

The man across from me on the bus had a small dog, a Corgi mix, in a carrier, and I looked at it longingly, the way most women eye babies. Outside the wind picked up. The roads were slick. The snow turned to hail, then back to snow again. Seattle doesn't get much snow or ice; urban legend has it that the city sold all of its snowplows to establish another park. Without plows, the roads stay sketchy until the ice and snow melt, or cars furrow a path.

We were on Aurora, passing Greenlake, when the windows of the bus went white. The bus skidded, cars honked, skidding their own curved courses, the fenced hedge and parked cars on our right got so close, but nothing touched. No screech of metal or thunk of trees. Everyone gasped, but it seemed safe enough when we righted ourselves. For a moment visibility returned and we could see the sex motels dividing Wallingford from Fremont and the ride went on as normal, though slowly, slowly on the fresh white road. Just before the bridge the bus signaled its stop.

This was where my look-alike usually exited, while I stayed on the bus until Broadway and 12th. She tucked her book into her bag, stood up, and swayed. Then she dropped her bag, and it slid under the seat behind her. As I watched I heard a crash, and then I don't really remember. Or maybe I do but I choose not to see. Our bus slid to a skittish stop at the start of the Aurora Bridge. Aurora's a suicide bridge into chilly Lake Union. Later I learned that the bus behind us hit a streak of ice and slid into us, pushing us, until our nose end slid over the guardrail.

What I remember is panic all around while I moved very calmly to the back of the bus. The front of the bus was gone, taking with it the girl and the driver. Split between seats, like a magician had sawed it in two. In front of me, three rows of seats and then nothing. I followed the crowd toward the back. Through all the screaming and shouting and dead white noise inside me, I heard the dog. It howled from its carrier, on the row of seats hanging? Dangling? above the bridge. Someone grabbed my hand but I shook away and stepped tightly, one foot in front of the other on an invisible rope. I picked it up, the carrier, and turned back, and as I passed the girl's bag, I picked that up too.

I didn't mean to take what wasn't mine. I just needed to do something, and salvage seemed shiny. I wasn't thinking clearly, I think I thought that what I took I intended to return.

Someone helped me jump off the bus, and someone tried to take the dog. I flung the girl's bag across my chest and grabbed the dog back. We gathered on the side of the road—there was nowhere else to go—and all talked at once into the snow. Someone stopped traffic, and then there were sirens, and soon a blanket over my shoulders. Again someone tried to take the dog. I refused, and in the end they let me take it in the ambulance, along with the girl's bag still slung over my chest. I had a headache, and felt as if I'd fallen, cramped and tense, but otherwise I seemed the same.

"What's your dog's name?" The EMT was trying to get me to relax.

Talking seemed too difficult. I covered my face with my hands.

"People forget their names all the time. Accidents do that. Don't worry. You're safe."

Later I noticed the nametag read Ely. That seemed like my dog's name, and so then it was.

When we got to the hospital everything got even more chaotic. Because I could walk they left me sitting in the waiting room, Ely in her crate, while the most serious injuries swung through the doors. After an hour I asked how much longer. The nurse looked stricken. Photographers clustered outside the emergency room entrance. A doctor emerged from the doors, wiping his hands on his scrubs.

Camera flashing, a photographer hustled his way inside. "Dr. Zulaski, can you give us an update? Anything?"

Dr. Zulaski shook his head.

The nurse stood up. "Not much longer." I recognized a few faces from the bus. Some people sat in groups, talking about the accident. Others detached, as if to forget. A couple sat side-by-side, whispering, his hand touching her shoulder, her hand touching his thigh; a tall man bent like a snapped tree held his head in his hands. A young woman cried silently while watching TV. One man bought Cheez-its and muttered some prayer, a few words before each cracker. Two small children sat on the floor with an older child, eating candy bars and watching TV. I could smell something unpleasant, and at first I thought I was bleeding. Then I realized that Ely had wet her crate. "I need to take my dog out for a minute. I'll be right back." The nurse looked down at Ely. "You have a dog? You can't have a dog in here. What was your name? Did you sign in?" I hadn't signed anything. At least forty of us had arrived at the hospital at once. "I'll be right back. I'm going to find someone to watch my dog." Outside it had stopped snowing. Without a hat my ears stung. I looked to see if Ely had a leash. She had a collar, but nothing else. I rummaged through the girl's bag, searching for a makeshift leash. This was the only time I felt guilty—the first time I reached in. I could feel hard and soft things, but nothing like rope. Then I felt a headset, with earplugs. Would earplugs be long enough for a leash? Not long enough. Something smooth—a wallet. I didn't hesitate, but opened it to find her license. *Masie Jones.* I put the wallet back. Something soft—stockings. An extra pair, black like her shoes. I opened Ely's crate and held her collar. Tied one foot of the stockings around it, then let her out. She rushed off while I raced to keep up. The emergency room opened onto a parking garage, which was filled with photographers and reporters. Someone approached me but I brushed him? her? off.

"I wasn't on the bus. It's my appendix."

He frowned and turned away.

Ely and I raced down the sidewalk and around the side of the building. There was a small grassy courtyard with an awning, so the grass wasn't so snowy and my ears weren't so cold. Ely peed and sniffed. I talked to myself. "Your name isn't Masie and this isn't your dog."

But Ely *felt* like my dog and Masie *felt* like my name. My old name was gone. I didn't plan to lie; that's the thing. It's not like I plotted and worked it all out. I didn't take the name Masie; the name took me. Ely took me, too, and then there we were.

"Ely," I called her, and she turned her head. "We're going home now." I opened my wallet to find out where we lived.

CHAPTER THREE

My new old apartment was in Wallingford. I wasn't taking any chances on another bus, so I called a taxi. When the driver picked me up, he wanted to talk about the crash.

"Must've been busy in there. A bus went over the Aurora Bridge. Five people dead, at least. Right into the water. Did you see 'em? The survivors?"

"Yeah. It was crazy."

"What were you in for?"

"My appendix."

"Me, too. Couple of years ago. Hurt like hell."

"This is it. You can let us off at this corner. Thanks."

It was a four-story brown-brick building set close to the street, concrete finials over the door like fleurs de lis, concrete planters on each side of an entrance filled with dead shrubs. But the door had no handles, no space for a key. After anxiously walking Ely up and down the block I turned the corner. The real door, keyed door, door with named buzzers faced 45th. It was propped open with an overturned bucket. And inside the hallway smelled like damp books and curry. Ely and I climbed the stairs, then turned left down the hall. 312 B was conveniently located next to 312 A.

I knocked on the door, and Ely barked.

Nothing.

I knocked again, waited, knocked. Then I rummaged through Masie's bag, and found a keychain with five keys. I tried three in the door before the fourth clicked the lock.

The door swung open, and Ely trotted into the room. Like she lived there.

A window stretched the length of the room, divided into one large glass panel flanked by two smaller panels. Old glass—real glass—without screens. Orange curtains and an orange rug. To the left of the window tucked into an alcove was a bed. To the right, a closet and a cramped bathroom without a door. To the left of the door, a galley kitchen. Hardwood floors, even in the bath. Cream-colored walls. No table, no desk.

Ely sniffed about. I was worried that Masie might have a cat or a bird, but nothing meowed or cawed. We seemed to be alone. I checked the closet. The clothes looked familiar, things I'd seen Masie wear, or things she might wear, if she wasn't dead.

It hit me suddenly. I was standing in a dead woman's apartment, holding onto her stockings, which were tied around the collar of a dead man's dog. Out the window, down the street, over the highway and above the bridge was a bus, hanging precariously over the water, and below, small boats dredging the lake for remains. If I turned on the television I'd see the names of the dead, maybe my name among them, while I stood here breathing, and no one knew.

I felt in my purse for my cell phone, thinking to call Joshua, but I couldn't even turn it on. What was in front of me seemed more real than anything ever had. This bed, with its deep blue comforter, green-and-white sheets frayed at the seams, seemed more real than our crisp gray sheets, our hospital corners. The clothes in the closet seemed more familiar than Joshua's neatly-pressed pants, each folded precisely in half, and hung over a wooden bar. Even the smells in Masie's apartment seemed like my life waiting to happen. I sat on the floor with my back against the bed. Ely curled at my feet, panting, then licked my hand.

The window was dark, which can mean anything in Seattle. I got up, stretched, and peered into Masie's kitchen. The clock said 2:06. I put water in a bowl for Ely and drank two glasses myself. From downstairs I could smell bread baking, and maybe Indian food. I opened Masie's refrigerator. A bottle of vinaigrette, two Styrofoam boxes of leftovers, soy creamer, a dozen apples, and five different kinds of cheese.

There was a loaf of bread on top of the refrigerator. I

made two cheese sandwiches with the least exotic-looking cheese. Ely and I ate, listening as traffic trundled down 45th.

Masie didn't have a TV, but she did have a radio. I'd be able to find out more about the accident on the news. Then it occurred to me that I had been in the accident, and knew more about it than any reporter ever would. What would I listen for? My name, dead or missing? Joshua's voice, pleading with me to come home?

Ely lay at my feet. I bent down and stroked her back. Then I heard the noise: footsteps. Keys. Someone stood fumbling outside our door. Ely looked up at me, one ear cocked, one folded over her eye. I could see she wanted to bark. "Good dog," I whispered.

The keys rattled, and then a voice: "Hi, honey." Someone shut the door across the hall. Everything went still, and the apartment flooded with traffic noises. I was on the bus. The bus had split in two.

I sat down, dizzy. It was happening all over again. Masie stood up, then she dropped her bag. When we slammed into the guardrail I saw her hit. Something bright, and silver, and the rest of her body. What I'd washed away while I walked to the front of the bus to pick up Ely in her crate, and to pick up Masie's bag, was blood. So much blood. The man with the dog hit the guardrail, too.

CHAPTER FOUR

Ely knew what I knew: about the blood, about the bodies. I don't know if she loved me right away. I think she just decided we should stick together. When I left a room, she did. If I stopped abruptly to look at something, she stayed with me there. On the street we'd been tethered, but loosely. She never strained at the stocking-leash. We had new names and a soft, rumpled bed.

Not long after I woke up from dreaming of the crash, still seeing the crash, still unable to imagine leaving Masie's apartment, Ely began to whine. I'd never had a dog before, not even as a kid. At first I didn't know what she wanted. You walk dogs, don't you? Yes, you do.

The tights I'd used as a leash lay like snakeskin by the door. I rummaged through Masie's closet to see if there was some more suitable lead. One of her dresses had a thin, flexible belt. I fastened this to Ely's collar. The weather outside hadn't gotten any better, so I took dry socks, a thick, fuzzy sweater, and a hat from the closet. I wasn't sure if Ely was the sort of small dog who needed clothing. She seemed pretty fat and sturdy, but just in case I took a t-shirt and wrapped it around her, tying it under her like a cape. As we walked down the hall, I heard a thud, and then someone opened the door to 312 D.

"What's up, Masie?" He was tall and thin, with short spiky dreads and horn-rimmed glasses. An odor of pot smoke hung by the door.

"Not much."

"See you got a dog. Thought you didn't like dogs?"

"I changed my mind."

"Yeah, you do that a lot, don't you? Hey, tell you what. I won't say anything to our dick of a landlord if you don't tell him about Monique."

"Deal."

"You heading out?"

"Yeah, I'm walking my dog."

He walked with Ely and me down the hall and outside. He talked about whatever he and Masie usually talked about. Apparently Masie sometimes went to hear his band and they were playing at the club this Thursday and was I coming and was I bringing Carlton?

So Masie had a boyfriend. Carlton. I hoped he didn't share her apartment. Clearly I looked enough like Masie to fool her neighbors, but what would I do about Carlton?

"Are you okay? You look tired or hungry or something."

"I just took a nap."

"Whatever. See you around." He hopped on the bus that pulled up to the curb.

The sound of the bus pulling away startled me. I pressed myself against the brick wall of a bakery while Ely pressed herself into my feet. Petting her head calmed us both down. "Good girl, Ely. Sit. Nice dog."

We started walking down Wallingford Avenue, past rows of immaculate bungalows. No one seemed to care that I'd almost died, that I'd stolen a dead girl's name and apartment. At the bottom of the hill was Gasworks Park. We stood among ruins and looked out at Lake Union. Ely wanted to climb Kite Hill, but I was worried if we stood on the sundial, we might be able to see the scene of the crash. Some part of me didn't believe it had happened because some part of me felt like I really was Masie, as if this life had been waiting for me all along.

On our way back to the apartment we stopped in at a grocery. I walked inside with Ely, as if it was the most natural thing to do. No way was I leaving her tied outside now that I knew how easy it was to steal a dog. She was such a good dog, too, so sweet and polite. I bought dog food, vegetable soup, wine, and chocolate. As he was adding up the sale, the cashier winked.

"Nothing for Carlton today, huh, Masie?"

What would Carlton want? "Pack of cigarettes."

"There you go."

"Give me a lighter, too, thanks."

"Anytime."

"See ya."

Ely and I walked back uphill. Inside Masie's apartment I dried Ely with a bath towel, gave her food and water, then worried over whether to take a shower. What if Carlton come home in the middle of my shower and thought I'd killed Masie and called the police? What if, what if. There were so many terrible scenarios. Anything could happen, really. But I was freezing, and tired, and still had blood in my hair.

The bathroom was tiny, so cramped there wasn't even a door. Just a curtain, black with white skulls. No tub, just a shower stall. When I stepped inside, the stall opened up because of the skylight. The shower told me more about Masie than the refrigerator. There was a candle in the soap dish, along with waterproof matches, and a waterproof radio on the wall. In a corner of the shower was a red plastic bucket filled with bars of fancy soap, shampoo, conditioner, shaving cream, and a woman's razor. I used purple soap to start, then switched to yellow speckled with orange and green. Everything smelled great, and above me the skylight glowed with sky. I washed my hair three times to get rid of the blood. As I rinsed off, Ely started barking.

I heard the door. A creak, and a slam. I slipped out of the shower, wrapped myself in a towel, and grabbed the only weapon I could find: Masie's razor. Then I tiptoed toward the curtain, and yanked it open.

Ely stood barking at a pile of mail that had fallen through the slot in the door. I put the razor back in the bucket, wrapped myself in the robe hanging on the wall, and sat on the floor to read Masie's mail.

CHAPTER FIVE

The first letter I opened was a bank statement. As I looked over Masie's finances I realized I was in fact looking at what I'd inherited. Because if I really was Masie, and not me, I couldn't take money out of my own account.

So this was it, then. This was what I had to work with. Our bank statements weren't especially distinctive. I had more money in savings, but Masie had more in checking. We both lived mostly hand-to-mouth. Until I got a job I would have to be careful. Unless, of course, I had a job, a job I could keep, in this guise, as Masie.

I left the rest of the mail on the floor and began searching Masie's apartment for evidence of her job. That was when something occurred to me, something that should've stuck out before. If Masie's apartment was in Wallingford, and she took the morning bus to her home, not her job, she must work skeleton shift somewhere. I'd assumed that she was going to work from the suburbs, like me, but Masie worked in the suburbs and lived in the city.

Her apartment was spare, as if spare was something she practiced. I couldn't find a single thing to indicate job, no job, or why the bus from Everett. Then I remembered the matches in the shower. *Shore Thing*. There was a bar just off the highway in Everett, a strip joint called *Shore Thing*. I'd been there once, with Joshua, on what could only be called a dare. He was shocked to learn I'd never been to a strip club. I was shocked at how easy it was to lie. In fact I'd worked in a strip club the year I turned eighteen, when I was living in Oak Harbor. I needed to move out of my mother's house when her boyfriend moved in and they started fighting. Joshua was so clean-cut, so tidy. It didn't pay to tell him the truth. So we went to *Shore Thing* and made fun of the dancers, of the waterproof matches they gave out with drinks.

Maybe we'd seen Masie dance that night. I didn't remember her, and I would've remembered. But maybe she wore a wig, or made herself into someone different the way I used to, the way girls do.

I went back to the pile of mail. There was a circular from the Wallingford Grocery, a catalogue for women's shoes, and the electric bill. There was also a letter, with no return address.

Opening the letter felt like a violation. Here I was, wearing Masie's robe, sitting on the floor of her apartment having rummaged her keys out of her stolen purse, and now I was worried about reading a letter? But there's something so private about ink on paper. I unfolded the cream-colored stationary and read:

> *Dear Masie,*
> *I miss you.*
> *Carlton*

Who was I fooling? Carlton would tell and I'd go to jail. Not so many miles away Joshua sat on the leather sofa in our excessively clean two-bedroom house watching the news. He would know by now that I was on the bus. He would know because I hadn't called. They wouldn't find my body, but they also wouldn't find me. Missing, and one day, presumed dead. I was already a file, bones in the water. I was the girl who didn't come home.

Leaving Joshua this way was cruel, but not entirely. It was cruel to lie, but perhaps less cruel than telling the truth. The truth was, I wasn't in love. I hadn't cared much for Joshua, only felt afraid of living alone. I hadn't known who I was, and he gave me a map. There were rules, and lines. Dinner at 6. The cruel hand of silence, of acceptance, his hand on my wrist.

I could call Joshua and tell him I was alive, that I'd survived the crash, but was leaving him anyway. I could tell him I'd changed my name to Masie and stolen a dog. I could tell him I never wanted to see him again and if I did, I'd pretend we were strangers.

Or I could disappear. He'd cry, my mother would console him, and they'd both get on with their lives. My mother would set broken planes aright and sleep with soldiers on leave from Iraq. Joshua would mourn, and quickly remarry. He'd marry Shelley, his office affair.

It wasn't that I didn't care for him, or my mother, or whatever friends I had at work. It's just that none of it felt like mine. I couldn't reconcile the life I had been leading with anything inside myself. As a child even I had spoken in the third person. It took years to train me out of this, but it was something I still believed. Lolita Lux just wasn't me, wasn't in me.

I ran my fingers through Ely's fur and stroked her ears. "Sit," I said, and she did. "Good dog." She looked worried, as if she was wondering what had become of her owner, or maybe she was worried I wouldn't hold on. "Don't worry, little dog. We're in this together. I won't let you go." I think she knew it was true.

Suddenly I heard the jingly chorus of a popular song coming from Masie's bag. Her cell phone must've been on all this time. I wondered if it was Carlton, and if it was his first call, or if he'd called while Ely and I were out walking. And why call, why not knock on the door? If I were Carlton, I'd race over to Masie's apartment. I'd pound on the door.

I looked at the phone. ST was calling. Probably wondering if I was showing up for my shift.

"Hello?"

"Masie, that you?"

"It's me."

"Good, good. We heard about, you know, the accident. On Aurora. You hear about it? Bus went over the bridge. Couple fatalities, couple folks missing. Anyway, good. You coming to work?"

"Look, I was on the bus. I'm okay but I can't make it tonight. I hurt my hand. Stitches and everything."

"Do you really need your hand to dance?"

"It's a blood thing."

"Gotcha." He hung up.

I walked over to the window. I could see into someone's apartment across the street. A naked body was brushing its teeth.

I called back. "Hi. It's Masie."

"Lemme guess. Your hand is magically cured."

"No. I quit."

His pause was a shrug. "I'll cut your last check and send it off in the mail."

It was that easy to send Masie's life in a new direction. Now I just had to find Carlton, and get a new job. But first I had to walk the dog.

Seattle's brighter at night than it is in the day. As I left the apartment, I crossed paths with 312D again.

"Carlton came looking for you. Said there was an accident on Aurora? Something about a bus going over the bridge. I said you were fine, and that you got a dog. But you should stop by the bakery in the morning because everybody seems to think you're dead."

"Is he coming over later?"

He laughed. "Dream on, right? I know the daysleeping thing must be hard for you guys. Carlton's probably asleep right now. And aren't you supposed to be working tonight?"

"I quit."

"About time. I heard the bakery's hiring. Can't pay as much as dancing but I bet you know how to amp up the tips."

"Thanks." It was like we were having a normal conversation, except that I didn't know his name or who my boyfriend was. "I'll check that out. First thing in the morning."

"Good night, Masie. I won't tell."

He means about Ely, I told myself. He won't tell about the dog. And I won't tell about Monique, whoever that is. But what if I slipped? What if I said something so wrong that 312D leaned in closer and noticed that I didn't have a scar on my cheek the way she did, or that I didn't wear her perfume?

What if we'd slept together (which seemed, given his tone, not entirely improbable) and I didn't remember? What if we were still sleeping together, maybe behind Carlton's back? What if I wasn't attracted to Carlton and had to dump him? Should I dump him over the phone, if I could find his number? What if he was hot, and was willing to accept this new and different Masie, given that old Masie was actually dead? What if he didn't notice? Would I like him if he didn't notice that I wasn't his girlfriend? How long could I go on fooling everyone and would I eventually freak out?

Dead is dead. I had to decide. I could say that I'd broken into Masie's apartment in a state of shock, which was true. Or I could say I thought the dog was hers, and went looking for her because I'd found her bag among the wreckage. I could say anything at this point, less than 24 hours after the crash. But time was passing. At some point, shock would turn into lying. My excuses wouldn't fly. And the more people involved in Masie's life, the more likely I'd get caught.

Suddenly I was too tired to sort out the strands of what I should do. I brushed my teeth with the toothbrush I kept in my bag, lifted Ely onto the pillow beside me, and to the tune of her snoring, slept.

CHAPTER SIX

I woke up with what felt like Joshua's feet laying heavily over my thighs. "Move it," I said roughly. I hated the way he sprawled in sleep.

But then the whimper, and bark, the strange bed with a bright blue comforter. Sun streamed in through orange sherbet curtains. I remembered the dog at my feet.

"Good girl, Ely." I rubbed her ears and she nuzzled my armpit. "We're going to make everything right today. Remember, I'm Masie, you're Ely. Let's go."

Ely gobbled some food and we walked a few times around the block. The bank clock read 8:07. I had a headache, probably from the crash but maybe also from missing my coffee. Usually I woke up at 5:30 and had two cups before I caught the bus.

Below Masie's apartment was a bakery. I'd stopped in months ago, when Joshua and I went to a matinee at the cinema a few blocks down. I'd gotten my usual shot in the dark, most likely; what I remembered was the cookie. Not peanut butter, but peanuts. Actual peanuts, hardly any dough, sweet and salty. Suddenly I was so hungry I could hardly see.

I opened the door to the bakery. Ely trailed along behind me, nose in the air, sniffing for treats. I decided to be one of those dog people who refuses to take no for an answer, and insists on bringing their pet everywhere. Ely was something. Extremely well-behaved, at least so far, although I figured she probably had her limits. There was no one behind the counter so I rang the bell.

A woman walked out from the kitchen wiping her hands on a floury apron. "Hi, Masie. You're early today. I haven't seen Carlton."

"Oh, I'm hungry is all. I'll have a peanut butter cookie and a shot in the dark."

She laughed. "That's funny."

I smiled back.

"What do you want?"

"A shot in the dark and a peanut butter cookie."

She frowned. Somehow I'd answered wrong.

"They aren't for me. They're for the dog."

"What's his name?"

"Ely. And she's a girl."

"Dogs love peanuts, but coffee and chocolate are fatal to dogs. If you're going to take care of Ely, you might want to read up. Google dog care, at least."

"The coffee's not for the dog. Just the cookie."

"You're weird today. First you're early, then you want coffee, then you want peanuts, which practically killed you a couple of months ago."

You are allergic to peanuts.

"I'll be sure not to eat the cookie. And the coffee's not for me at all."

"See you later."

"Are you hiring?"

"You're too much." Untying her apron, she walked around to the front of the counter. "Do you really want to work with your ex?"

My ex works here—Who?

"Why not?" Ely wagged her tail, like she thought this was all hilarious.

"Michael says we're looking for morning help. But you've got a job, Masie. We can't match that in tips."

"I quit last night." As I said it, I had a feeling of pride: it was true. I wasn't making this part up.

"Did Carlton push you?"

"It was my idea. Carlton doesn't know."

"Oh my god. You got a dog. You quit your job. Now you want to work here, with me and Michael. And you look different. Are you drunk?"

"I gotta go. But I'm serious about the job."

"Suit yourself. I'll let Michael know."

Ely and I walked around the corner before I split the cookie between us. Then I sipped my coffee and tried to sort things out.

I am allergic to peanuts.
I dated someone at the bakery.
Carlton meets me at the bakery.
I don't drink coffee (not now or not ever?).

The last one was going to have to change. I could handle a peanut allergy. But no coffee? Not possible. Ely seemed pensive. I wondered if she was putting her new life together, too, smelling new street corners, adjusting to new food and new commands. It was 9 am. I hadn't checked my cell phone once. It seemed like I should listen, at least. I owed Joshua the thought of his call.

But back at the apartment when I turned on my cell and saw the message icon, I couldn't do it. 28 calls. It would take hours to listen to them all. Everyone thought I'd died in the crash. I had died in the crash. My new name was Masie. Besides, what if the cell phone company could tell that I'd checked my messages? Shouldn't I throw the phone away?

I pried the phone apart with a knife, ran each piece under water in the sink, then wrapped them in paper towels and put them in my purse. I'd throw them in a dumpster next time I took Ely out.

Masie's closet was full of dresses, mostly vintage, and little sweaters with sequins and bows. I picked out a blue dress that almost fit; it was a little too big, so I tied the belt tightly. Then a black sweater with sparkly birds. Black stockings, and my own black shoes. I brushed my teeth and put on my own dark red lipstick.

On Masie's refrigerator were photos of Bettie Page. I wanted to look like her before and after. Before, when she reveled in the scenes she set, and after, when she found God and vanished into her private heaven.

I re-did my lipstick, brushed my hair, and straightened my sweater. My coat was wrong for the outfit, but Masie's vintage coat was gone, with her, underwater. Lake Union. And what if they found her body? And what if they found I'd stolen her name? I cycled through all of these questions at near-regular intervals.

When Ely and I walked into the bakery, the woman in the floury apron was making espresso for two older women and a young woman with a child in a stroller. The child reached for Ely with sticky fingers, then dropped a cinnamon roll.

Ely dragged the roll across the floor and set it at my feet like prey. The child started to cry.

"Your little boy just dropped his roll and I'm afraid my dog's got it."

The young woman snapped her head in my direction. "Dogs don't belong in restaurants," she said.

This didn't phase me. Seattle was full of conflicts between new money and laid back old ways, between people who bought stock in Starbucks and people who worked part-time at Starbucks for the health insurance because professional Frisbee golf didn't pay very well. Somewhere between my own old and new, in my stolen vintage clothes, with my stolen little dog, I wasn't sure I was old hippie Seattle, pre-dot com, but I certainly wasn't this uptight brand of new.

CHAPTER SEVEN

There were metal chairs outside the café, so Ely and I waited for New Seattle to leave. At the corner of 45th and Wallingford two crows wrestled over leftover pizza. It was cold outside, but not snowing or raining. Just clear, with a sky the same blue as my new bed.

The bakery's bell rang, and New Seattle trundled out of the shop with her stroller and grandmothers in tow. Ely and I promptly reclaimed the bakery, splitting a croissant and making small talk with Floury Apron Woman.

"How soon are you hiring?"

"You're serious?"

"Dead. Will you talk to Michael?"

"Masie, we both know Michael will hire you. It's not about Michael."

I was trying to think of a reply vague enough to mean something, yet direct enough to elicit more information, when an enormous bouquet of flowers walked in and sat at my table.

"Carlton, you're such a sweetheart," Floury Apron Woman said.

"I try, Jenny. I really try."

The flowers let me be Masie a few moments longer. I dreaded the moment to come, the moment when Carlton would notice whatever was too much or not enough about me. Whatever wasn't Masie.

Ely barked at Carlton's feet. Carlton stood up. "C'mon. Let's go back to your apartment." He held out his hand, smiling at me.

We walked around the corner and climbed the stairs. Carlton held the flowers while I unlocked the door. Ely ran into the apartment and jumped on the bed.

"What's the dog's name?"

"Ely."

"Does Masie know?"

I looked at the floor.

"Not to be pushy, but who are you? Is this some kind of joke? Where's Masie? And when is she coming back from wherever she went?"

"It's a long story."

"So start."

"If I tell you what's going on, will you promise not to tell?"

"You're freaking me out. Are you Masie's sister? Who the hell are you?" Carlton walked to the window and looked at the apartment across the way. "Did Masie send you to break up with me?"

"She's not breaking up with you."

"I'll just wait here until she gets back."

"I wouldn't do that."

"Why not?"

"Masie's dead."

Carlton backed away from me. "You're wearing her clothes. What is this? I'm calling the police."

"It was an accident. We were on the bus that went over the Aurora Bridge. Masie was in front of me. Her seat hit the guardrail. She—I saw her. I can't stop seeing her. Everything just came apart, and she was dead, and the front of the bus went into the lake."

"You're lying."

"I saw it happen."

"Who are you?"

"Just a girl on the bus."

One of us was crying. I thought it was Carlton but it turned out to be me. I wiped my face on the sleeve of Masie's sweater and tried to explain. "Masie and I took the 7:13 out of Everett. I didn't know her name. We never talked. I just knew we looked alike. The bus skidded a couple of times but I wasn't scared. I mean, a bus isn't like a car. Buses don't seem fragile. The accident still doesn't seem real, but it's the realest thing ever. I saw everything, and I can't stop seeing it. Masie died. The guy who was carrying Ely died. Everyone was screaming and there was blood in my hair and I just took the dog and Masie's bag and climbed out of the bus. I went to the hospital, but there were too many people and the cameras were terrible. I had to leave but I couldn't go back to Joshua. I couldn't call him. I can't. He wasn't the right life for me and now I finally have a chance to get out. People just started calling me Masie. I'm sorry she's dead."

"You can't just steal Masie's life."

"I didn't steal it. She happened to me."

"You're crazy. You're making this up."

"I wish I was, but the crash really happened."

Carlton balled his hands into fists. "You're crazy. Only a lunatic would play games with a dead person's stuff. Who are you, really?"

"I didn't mean anything bad. She isn't using her life so I am."

Carlton said nothing, stared. Stepped closer to me, twelve inches, ten inches, five, his eyes level with mine. "She isn't using her life? What does that even mean?" The first sentence spoken, the second yelled.

"I'm sorry," I said. "I didn't—"

"Where'd he come from?" Carlton asked, motioning toward Ely.

"The guy who was carrying her is dead too. What was I supposed to do, just let her sit there crying in her cage until the rest of the bus went over the guardrail?"

He started crying. "I was falling in love. We had just started seeing each other, just started having sex."

"I'm sorry. I don't have anyone." I looked at him, his strong hands, slumped shoulders. I looked at his adam's apple, neck stubble, asymmetrical eyebrows, the tenuous history of acne scarring his cheeks. What would it be like to kiss him? To lie under him? On top? What would it be like, his brush of moustache, soft lower lip? Would he taste like petrichor, a ball point pen, some trace of garlic, or hint of stale coffee, stale beer? Would it be something I remembered when he put his arms around me? How warm would he feel? I held my hands at my side, but I wanted to reach for him.

"Maybe you're lying," he said. "You stole her purse."

"She was dead before she went over the bridge," I said. "I'm sorry."

"This is sick. Now what? Am I supposed to keep your secret? You get to be Masie and I have to lie, too?" His eyes rimmed red with wet.

I said nothing while I tried to look at him, hold his gaze, will my eyes teary too. I thought of the dog and she whined and I hummed softly until the sound turned to sobs. I wanted him to stay, to sit down, to drink tea. I wanted to feel the inside of his palms on my face. He shook his head softly, walked to the door, and closed it behind him.

Sleet struck the window in a steady patter. Carlton was right, I was crazy. I'd have to call Joshua and tell him the truth. Then I'd have to call the police, if Carlton hadn't first, and tell them about Masie.

But I was going to sleep first. And I wasn't going back, not to Joshua. Never again. And I was going to keep Ely, no matter what anyone said.

When I woke the sky was heavy and gray and the air had stilled and the white noise of traffic filtered up from the street.

THE MAN ON THE BUS

It happens all the time. I meet you, or another just like you, in one of the bars on Capitol Hill. You aren't wearing a ring and neither am I, but I can tell you're married by your downcast eyes.

When we leave the hotel or your clandestine apartment, there's a man in a car parked two blocks away. He trails one of us home and sends the bill to your wife. By then I know more about you than she ever will.

There's a subtle difference between stealing and rescue. One makes you a thief and the other, a saint. Take my neighbor's dog, for instance: chained to a fence. Sometimes when I walk past their house, I imagine the feeling of cutting that chain. I'd scoop up the dog and ride out of town. Find someone to love it, let it sleep on their bed.

When I opened the refrigerator this morning, the juice was touching a bottle of beer. Worse, an apple was touching the butter. It took five minutes to move everything around, set a perimeter so nothing touched anything else.

Before I leave the house, before I fall asleep, before I think of you, I check the stove. I wash my hands, check the door, check the dryer. Set the alarm and set it again.

It goes on forever, and it's not just me. All over this country we're trapped in our homes. It's a Victorian illness: domestic, detailed. There's a feminine tinge to this form of decay.

This is why I won't bring you home. I can't turn it off until I enter your world. In the hotel, in your apartment, I'm free of the impulse. I can stop holding the plane in the air.

A year ago I should've learned my lesson. No more hotels. No more married men. You were silent as I laced my shoes, as I slipped on my jacket and smoothed back my hair. My car was parked in the hotel garage, poorly-lit for a downtown address. As I unlocked the trunk, I heard footsteps behind me. Then a fist, and my vision dissolved.

I never saw my attacker's face, but he smelled of soap, cigarettes, and starched linen. The smell reminded me of closeness, of someone I knew. His fist smelled like you.

After the attack I was in surgery for hours. When I woke, the doctors warned I might lose my sense of smell. Weeks of blood, bandages, and boredom. My nose seemed fine when the gauze was removed.

Slowly I lost my taste for sugar. I bought a cake to be sure. A birthday cake in the shape of a doll, white frosting like a lazy bride.

I lifted her skirt with the prongs of my fork.

I don't smell anything at all anymore.

Tie a dog to a chain and it slowly goes mad, collar growing into its skin. My neighbors must hate this dog they feed. It shivers when I pass the fence, curled into a ball, the end of its rope.

I make my living tracking smells, but not with my nose. A code smell is a warning, the start of a trail. A good programmer tracks code smells instinctively, keeping an open mind about what waits at the end of the trail.

Like many programmers, I work from home, for a famous company whose name I never mention. It's not worth the eye rolls and assumptions that come with that name, especially the misconception that I must be rich. I live in Everett, which sums up my financial status nicely. Everett's one of those cities that won't let you back on the highway after you exit.

Working from home means I set my own hours, but it also means I work when I'm sick. I can wear pajamas, but I can't share jokes. The only gossip I know is about me and you.

I've always relied on smell in sex. Now I fear I'm a clumsy lover. I need to understand how I missed your rage: the scent you covered with ash and fast hands.

This morning a detective drove past my house. I watched his car trample leaves in the gutter. In the realm of bad habits, my checking's benign. If a life is destroyed, at least it's my own.

Researchers think counting and checking is a postmodern twist on evolution. Our ancestors' capacity for adrenaline has become overdeveloped in this age of chemicals, artifice, and stress. The voice in my head that says I left the stove on is the same voice Neanderthals relied on when the forest caught fire or a bear stumbled into their cave. Except that my voice never shuts off. It codes everything panic.

I grew up in Eastern Washington, which is like the Midwest. Outsiders think of this state as gay Mecca, but it's as easy to die in Spokane as Detroit.

When I was younger I moved, restless, blaming each new apartment for my habit. When I first moved into a new space

I could sleep without checking the stove. Over time my habits became embedded in my surroundings. Appliances glowed with the harm they might do.

When I bought my condo, I thought things would be different. I thought the need to stay close would cancel the fear. But checking's like kudzu—something I manage. I prune back my habit and my habit returns.

My neighbors don't know how lucky they are to have a dog so loyal it still looks their way. I don't know who they are, my neighbors. I don't know why they have a dog. An expensive dog, too, by what's left of its fur. A Corgi, the favorite of queens.

If you don't want your dog, find someone who does. If you don't want your wife, unfasten her chain. I don't understand the false promise of home. My promises are real, which is why they're rare.

When I promised I'd call you, I meant it. Your wife answered the phone, which struck me as odd. You don't give out your landline if you're having affairs. Then again, maybe she answers your cell.

We talked for a while, your wife and I. She seemed interested in what the bank had to say. Your credit card must have been stolen, she mused. Those hotel bills couldn't be yours.

I shouldn't be loyal to you, but I am. I'm still hunting for you, the feel of your fist. If I can just forget the low hum of your voice, I might meet him tomorrow in a crowded café.

Across a sea of laptops I notice his eyes. He mouths hello. I push back my chair.

Later, over dinner, he turns off his phone.

No email. No Twitter. We're too busy live.

When I wake up in the hotel, his pillow is empty. The window's open. Rain drums the sill. He's sitting in the armchair, smiling. "Late sleeper," he says, and slides back into bed.

But what do I know about love, about marriage?

I can't even steal a dog.

Your wife called again. I thought I heard barking in the background. I couldn't imagine you with a dog, or a dog putting up with your fist, your tight cuffs.

"What kind of dog do you have?" I asked.

"I'd like a dog, but that's just the twins crying."

This weekend my car broke down on the Hill. I woke up alone in a shiny hotel and walked for hours, past the bricks of the U. No one would fix my car on a Sunday. I had it towed to Ballard by a taciturn Swede.

I love a fast car, a smooth ride down the highway. Without my car, I'm missing a limb. I took the express bus back to Everett, drenched in the feeling I'd forgotten my keys.

I know where you live because your wife told me. She offered to meet me, compare notes on your lies. It doesn't even feel like betrayal. She knows the beginning and I know the end.

Your wife's name is Elizabeth, Eli for short. Convenient: in bed you cry out a man's name. She says she'll let you go, and I believe her. We don't ask what you want. We both already know.

I told your wife I'd meet her tomorrow. Catch the bus to the city. A little brunch in Queen Anne. Then I'll pick up my car and drive back to Everett. By the time you get home, she'll have re-keyed the doors.

Before I lost my sense of smell, I could predict rain or snow by the scent of the weather. Now I look at the sky, and guess at the clouds.

My neighbor's dog shivers at the back of his crate.

RELOCATION PROGRAM

Autumn's the time for faking your death. Piles of leaves, loose threads on red sweaters. Early November in the Arboretum. Orange and ocher. The occasional gold.

I take photos. Stock. It's a day job, a night job. Everyone likes a white cat, a blue moon. That morning I shot straight through lunch. Got halfway to dinner when I heard my name.

Except the name, while mine, wasn't meant for me. It meant me, but not me in a stranger's soft voice. The voice was pleading with the name for mercy. I did what I do without thinking: took aim.

The photo meant I had to leave town. Simple as that; it wasn't even a question. So on casual Friday I faked my own death. Then I went running and beat my best time. Sometimes fake feels better than real. When I was a kid, I smoked candy cigars.

Kayla knew a guy at the morgue. She worked for a dentist so he had her on speed dial. One afternoon we were at her apartment when she got a call about a mystery corpse.

"Dental records," she shrugged. "Just a Doe. Do you have a twin?"

"Why do you ask?"

She held up her phone.

The face on her phone was my face, but dead.

Orange and ochre. The occasional gold. The bamboo beds light up with the sky. This is the hour they talk about.

I shot a deer pacing through red light. I ran over a doe.

"John," she called me, as she settled in my lap, a fiver between her teeth, though I'd meant to leave a ten.

Autumn's the name she gave me, auburn hair, fake tits, an inscrutable smile. She wants the money, needs the money, loves me loves me loves the square brick of my shoulders, my uneven hair. We started where?

I'm in my own relocation program. I'm in my own green velour chair. Everyone likes a fat cat, Russian blue. Everyone loves the moon. Seen nine ways through an empty tree, nine ways in the water. In stripes and in diamonds and still.

Ten pages missing from my diary. Bite marks in the cover that don't match mine. Teeth that weren't meant for me, name them: bicuspid and canine. My name wasn't meant for me: lawncare, outstretch, parent or guardian, sheepskin, lover, the loved, beloved, Winter. Anticipation of snow in my hair.

But the creature in the brush backtracks across the empty road where only the white moon watches. And hammers fall somewhere, nails shot back in the gun. The screws come loose and the house yields. The house yields, and the missing crawl back into their skin.

ACKNOWLEDGEMENTS

Carol would like to thank her friends and family. Special thanks to Kelly and love to Elizabeth.

Elizabeth would like to thank friends, family, collaborators, all those who make worlds possible, especially Carol Guess, my collaborator in everything.

Kelly would like to thank her family: Gus and Audrey Magee-Kenney, Joy Langone, Tim Magee, Cassie Quest, and Erin Magee for their love and support. Also friends and fellow collaborators, Carol Guess, Elizabeth Colen, and Kami Westhoff.

We would like to thank our students and colleagues at Western Washington University. Special thanks to Holly Andres (http://www.hollyandres.com) for allowing us to use her photograph on the cover. Special thanks to Justin Daugherty, Matthew Fogarty, and all at Jellyfish Highway Press.

Many thanks to the publications where some of these stories first appeared: "Amnesiac Lung" in *Whiskey Island;* "Damage Control" in *Ilanot Review*; "Struck" in *Glassworks*; "The Storm Grower" in *Sugared Water*; "Varda" in *New South*; "Your Sick" in *Anomalous Press*; and "Zero Fever" in *Mason's Road Literary Journal.*

ABOUT THE AUTHORS

Elizabeth J. Colen is the author of poetry collections *Money for Sunsets* and *Waiting Up for the End of the World: Conspiracies*, flash fiction collection *Dear Mother Monster, Dear Daughter Mistake*, long poem / lyric essay hybrid *The Green Condition*, and forthcoming novel in prose poems *What Weaponry*.

Carol Guess is the author of fifteen books of poetry and prose, including *Darling Endangered*, *Doll Studies: Forensics*, and *Tinderbox Lawn*. In 2014 she was awarded the Philolexian Award for Distinguished Literary Achievement by Columbia University. Her most recent book, *With Animal*, was co-written with Kelly Magee and published by Black Lawrence Press in 2015. She teaches in the MFA program at Western Washington University.

Kelly Magee is the author of *Body Language*, winner of the Katherine Anne Porter Prize for Short Fiction, and *With Animal*, co-written with Carol Guess. Her work has appeared in *Gulf Coast*, *Kenyon Review*, *Crazyhorse*, *Ninth Letter*, *Passages North*, *Nimrod*, *Hayden's Ferry Review*, and others. She teaches in the creative writing programs at Western Washington University.

Jellyfish Highway Press is
postindustrial bioluminescence;
we're abyssal gigantism.

Jellyfish Highway Press
www.jellyfishhighway.com
Atlanta, GA